Long Dark River Casino

G. Louis Heath

AuthorHouse™
1663 Liberty Drive
Bloomington, IN 47403
www.authorhouse.com
Phone: 1-800-839-8640

© 2009 G. Louis Heath. All rights reserved.

No part of this book may be reproduced, stored in
a retrieval system, or transmitted by any means
without the written permission of the author.

First published by AuthorHouse 5/12/2009

ISBN: 978-1-4389-7999-1 (sc)

Printed in the United States of America
Bloomington, Indiana

This book is printed on acid-free paper.
Cover photo is courtesy of Dr. Carl Robinson, English Department,
Ashford University, Clinton, Iowa.

For the students, faculty, and staff of Ashford University, one of the finest academic communities in the United States.

One
....

"Who is going to gamble at a casino called 'Long Dark River'?" lamented Ralph Kilen, Quinlan, Iowa city manager extraordinaire, as he sat back in his naugahyde executive chair in the empty council chambers—empty save for Kim Nevins, the director of the local chamber of commerce who had proposed the name.

"Who?" she retorted rhetorically. "Why everybody." She paused, adding, "At least plenty of people. Plenty enough to keep the marks coming in and parting with their money."

Ralph parted his hands in his keeled-back position, as if gravely measuring something. "But where in tarnation did you get 'Long Dark River'? It sounds so forbidding. It almost sounds philosophical." He swiveled slightly to square up to Kim who sat in a chair

G. Louis Heath

three councilpersons' spaces to his right. "Philosophy will drive away gamers. Especially dark philosophy."

Kim smiled resolutely, a smile of defiant determination. "This river that runs by Quinlan, is both long—after all, it is the Mississippi—and dark—after all, all manner of tragedy have marred every mile of it." She extracted a stick of gum from her purse and began unpeeling the wrapper, as if for dramatic effect, to underscore her words. "Long, dark river seems right to me. It is different, not bright like most casino names. It will be a niche for us, just the name. People like different in entertainment venues, which is what the casino will be."

Ralph exhaled forcefully, running the name in zippered neon through his mind's eye. "It is kinda Freudian to me. I like that. Yes, I can get used to Freudian dark. The river over beyond our flood wall, under its massive currents, in its murky depth conceals secrets, in a certain way, similar to the darkest, deepest grooves of homo sapiens' brain."

"I agree," observed Kim, wadding up her gum wrapper. "You make the river seem like a form of sentient life. That's what I want to get across in the name. The sense of risk posed by a river's life."

"And gambling certainly is risky," opined Ralph. "You can ruin yourself in a casino."

"Which is what makes my name just right." Ralph nodded. "We need to propose this name to the Wild River Corporation board at the meeting Tuesday evening."

Long Dark River Casino

Kim popped the gum into her mouth and smiled. As she did so, Jim the Janitor, aka Jim Brotherton, Ph.D., also an adjunct at Quinlan University atop the limestone bluffs overlooking town, followed his vacuum cleaner into the council chambers. At first oblivious to the presence of Kim and Ralph, he nozzled over a few square feet of bland patterned carpet, until he applied the suction hose to the very foot of Kim, who burst outlaughing. That Jim, she thought, so abstracted from reality, he has to vacuum me in order to discover my presence. "What are you doing, Jim? I am not carpet," she said cheerily, in a joking tone.

Jim pulled up short, suddenly aware of Kim. He gazed at her, blinking, as if awaking from a dream. And soon he descried Ralph, too. He bumbled, "Gee, you are here. I didn't see you."

"Apparently," intoned Ralph evenly. "We are in here discussing the new casino."

Kim added, "And we think we just came up with a great name. Wanna hear it?"

Jim nodded, his face inexpressive (as it always seemed to be).

"It is The Long Dark River Casino," she said portentously. "Whaddya think?"

Jim scratched his head, tentatively in the manner of a failed academic who had been déclassé into the proletariat, a janitor's job (which he did not hate as much as people said, because he had always regarded himself as part of the working class, the vanguard of the future). After a prolonged silence, he observed, "Sounds different anyway. It's not postmodern, but it is different, very different when you consider you're putting a philosophical moniker on a casino. As to whether I actually like it, I need to think on it."

Ralph challenged, as Jim stood poised at his vacuum in the demeanor of a professor at his podium, "Well, if you aren't sure about liking it, is there anything about it you don't like?" He had taught high school a year before becoming a city manager, and he knew something of how to get discussion going, even with a self-absorbed Ph.D. manqué.

Casting a glance up toward the fluorescent lights of the teal stucco ceiling, Jim rubbed his chin thoughtfully. "Dark doesn't turn me on," he replied. "It doesn't seem very American, to call a gambling venue dark. Dark is more for Europe, especially the French." He paused. "Y'know, I did my Ph.D. dissertation in France. So, I oughta know whereof I talk."

"You did a dissertation in France. That's fascinating," put in Kim. "What was it about?"

"Semiotics, signification, especially Michel Foucault. I really got into that stuff. It was not so much dark or light, as a manifestation of otherness."

Ralph clapped his hands loudly. "Maybe we could call the casino the Otherness Casino. We could drawn an other-oriented crowd or no crowd at all."

Kim smiled, then chuckled. "Works for me," she said dryly.

"The Long Dark River and Otherness Casino. That settles it," proclaimed Ralph. The Wild River Corp will rave over this concoction of a name."

Jim the Janitor did not smile. He never did. But Ralph and Kim thought they detected a soupcon of grandeur in his fully upright mien. Though he might be low on the academic totem pole, a mere adjunct at local Quinlan University, his research in Paris and environs had just lit a big light bulb of an idea, elevating him, at least temporarily, to a plane above the vacuum and broom!

Two

Kim and Ralph drove along the levee road that ran along the Mississippi River as it passed by Quinlan. (Not "through," as the other side of the river was occupied by Shelby, Illinois, home to a major seed corn company and an ethnic enclave of Danes with German names—the descendants of immigrants from Schleswig-Holstein.)

Ralph opined as the summer heat and humidity off the River tested his Camry's a/c, "I bet the Schleswig-Holsteiners will gamble at a casino called The Long Dark River and Otherness Casino. It's a complex name, like a lot of German words."

"And complex like Danes with Schleswig-Holstein names," added Kim.

A shorebird glided above the car. A few moments passed as the pair fell into silence. Elliptically, Ralph asked, "Seriously, why is Jim a Ph.D. working as a janitor for the city."

"No one knows for sure, but there are some stories floating around. He's been a janitor for fifteen years. He got on recently to teach a course at Quinlan University. Clearly something went wrong big-time in his career for him to end up where he is. He never even landed a full-time teaching job from which he got fired. Nobody cared to hire him. And the why of that is the nub and rub and hub of his sucking on your toes with a vacuum cleaner." Kim glanced at the shorebird landing on riprap along the river. "Like I said, there are stories."

"Do they have anything to do with his being so rigid? Or is it shyness?" Kim turned up the a/c a notch. "He seems to be so detached from reality. It's a wonder he can even hold down a zombie-pushes-broom job!"

"That Otherness suggestion just points up his problem. Who else would suggest something so weird?"

"Well, there is Dr. Gary Klemetson, the sociologist up at Quinlan. He's weird, unique might be a better word. I saw him essaying into the verdant Otherness a couple weeks ago, birdwatching. I saw him not far from here. He had his glasses on some sort of shorebird. Looked like an avocet to me."

Ralph joked, "Perhaps we can call the casino The Long Dark River, Otherness, and Avocet Casino."

"Dr. Klemetson might find that a bit much! I certainly do!" said Kim.

"Yeah, that is too long for a neon sign...unless you zipper the neon around the entire casino. That might work."

"We can try all the names on the Wild River Casinos Corp and see what works for them. The new marketing science of 'branding' is a strange and protean field that can yield unexpected results..." She let her words trail off.

"Like our name and variations thereof for the casino," continued Ralph.

Kim arched her eyebrows, to emphasize her words. "We need to bring Gary Klemetson into this. The naming is becoming possibly an event of social significance. We need the counsel of that sociologist-birdwatcher extraordinaire. He can maybe infuse meaning into the sordid commercial act of ripping off people through the legalized method of gaming. This is a project for Dr. Social Philosopher himself."

Ralph stopped to allow people exiting a summer play to cross. "Indeed, Prof G, the Social Philosopher, can add a layer of meaning to the numbers racket that can transform Quinlan."

"You took a class from him, I can tell," observed Kim. "You sound a lot like him. A real mimic."

Ralph grinned, "I got an A in his Social Meanings class."

The playgoers finished crossing the broad avenue atop the floodwall, and Ralph eased the car ahead, picking up modest speed as the Quinlan minor league baseball ballpark appeared to his left. "I think a small

Midwestern university town might make for a nice social laboratory. Dr. Klemetson can help us."

"And Jim the Janitor may provide a good fallback Ph.D. consultant."

"I can see us transforming Quinlan through the new casino."

It was now four in the afternoon and the sun beat down ferociously on the Camry that seriously tested the a/c. Kim looked at Ralph, who quickly returned her stare, then withdrew it as he returned his attention to navigating the road. After a prolonged silence, he said under his breath, "I think we are onto something big here. The Long Dark River, Otherness, and Avocet Casino."

"Works for me. Let's see if the Wild River people will go for it."

In the river, in the near-distance, some local boys were swimming, to ward off the heat and stay away from home another hour, or more, if possible. Ralph could see it was Jack Strang, a neighbor's kid and some other kid he either did not recognize or had never laid eyes on. "The Casino will provide for their future," he said grandly. "Not only money, but meaning, and we'll find out what that means."

"We'll build something for Quinlan that helps those kids. They need a future that is beyond the Mississippi, yet of it."

Kim looked at her watch, "Time to eat. Let's stop at the Organic Café. Their food is very healthy."

Ralph swung a left turn, and headed for the Organic. He loved their food. He felt healthier eating it. And he enjoyed Kim's company as he did so. He and she seemed to be alike in important ways. She was a good friend and sometimes helpmeet, though he would never entertain marrying her. That was out of the question, given his past and how it might get in the way.

Three

Professor Gary Klemetson sat back in his office chair at Quinlan University and contemplated the cemetery of Franciscan friars and sisters that flanked the Social Science Building. He liked viewing the dead, for it gave him a sense of superiority. What had they done wrong to die? Irrational as the thought was, he could never put it out of his head when he viewed the stolid, granite tombstones of the departed religious. Perhaps it was the heretic endemic in him that would never subside.

He held his arms benevolently toward the cemetery, as if in respect to the founders and sustainers of the University. He respected them deeply for all his sociological cynicism. After all, the friars and the sisters were nothing if but group-oriented. The social good did indeed walk in a surplice over a cassock as well as in a coif atop a habit, both outfits unmercifully hot on an Iowa summer's day. He certainly could appreciate the decedents' penchant for self-mortifying misery just on the issue of apparel alone, as he glanced down at his Quinlan University T-shirt, navy-blue Bermuda shorts, and huaraches. It was mid-July and keeping this side of a heat stroke was the 64-year-old Prof's pre-eminent goal for this particularly chthonic, humid day.

Dr. Klemetson had been hatching a clever idea for some time. It revolved around parlaying his research on the Tama, Iowa settlement of the Meskwaki Indians into absorbing some of their casino profits. He was tired of doing great research resulting in acclaimed monographs and books that only further put him into straitened circumstances. After all, he had thoroughly gained the confidence of the tribal council and most the informants who were participating in his current ethnographic study. It should not prove a summer lodge too far to get them to unwittingly help him augment his retirement nest egg into a piggybank that would ease him into a comfortable retirement. The Meskwaki owed him that; he had done so much for them, substantiating their legal and cultural claims to this and that and whatnot and whatfor. He had served them long and hard and there should be some sort of payback in it for him.

Every Meskwaki received a monthly allowance, drawn from the casino profits. Each month, a substantial check. He could sure use one of those, too, every month. He had shared his intellect and field research with the tribe. They should share back.

He studied a nuthatch winding up a tree trunk that knelt benevolently over the cemetery. That bird was another fool like himself: a workaholic. "Indeed!" he hissed. His mind was operating in overdrive as to how to effect a transfer of casino money to himself. He hated to do this. But at age 64, it was high time to stop thinking like a hybrid sociologist, anthropologist, and philosopher. It was indeed far overdue that he start asserting himself as the #1 priority. In a word, it was time for greed.

A bright idea came to the Professor, and he exclaimed, "Nuthatch!"

At that moment the nuthatch took flight, affixing himself— it was clearly a male nuthatch; any fool could tell that by the pattern of colors!—to a nearby Norwegian pine just outside the cemetery.

Four

Sam Sixkiller was closing up the tribal office at the Meskwaki settlement for the day. It had been an uneventful day because no one from the progressive mixed-blood faction of the tribe had either vandalized the relatively new, modern structure, nor had they seized it and locked out the traditionalists (as the progressive leader Jonathan Sleeping Horse had threatened to do in retaliation for the traditionalists doing that to them four years back). As he locked the twin glass-and-aluminum entry doors, Sam cast his usual wary eye over the immediate environs. He cocked his head, and tuned an ear to any interesting sound that might come his way. He stood in a tensile pose for quite a while, straining to hear auditory attention-getters that might prompt him to get on his cell phone and call for backup.

Long Dark River Casino

That was how the bastard dirty progressives operated. They'd pull any dirty trick they pleased, or could pull off, in order to harm the supporters of a hereditary chief for the tribe, a practice that had ended over 70 years before with the Indian Reorganization Act, but which a good portion of the tribe wanted to reinstate. After all, if they did not act like real Meskwakis soon, the casino that had looted them out of poverty would also lift the very scalp of their Indian-ness. And that would be the worst thing that could happen, even worse than death.

Sam cocked his head ever more attentively, homing in on the random sounds of a hot summer evening. Is that chirping a cricket? Or is it Jonathan Sleeping Horse snoring off a Choctaw beer or making inept stealthy sounds, malevolently intent on mayhem? He was not sure. The casino sickness, the white man's disease of greed, had wrought strange things on Sleeping Horse. Once fast buddies at the tribal school and later at South Tama High, they were now avowed strangers, avoiding each other like cholera or smallpox. That hurt still, but Sam had over the years come to realize that friendships die like people, and that it was best to move on to new acquaintances and friends rather than attempt to revivify a thoroughly maimed relationship.

Why, hell, he thought, it was all seasonal, this casino stuff. Casinos had been sprouting in Iowa for two decades but they would fade someday like over-marketed vices everywhere. And the sooner the better, because it didn't ease his anger at all that a new casino was now setting footings for preliminary construction over near Quinlan. That made him sick. How long would this gambling expansion go on against the wishes of the Meskwaki manitous, or spirits. He shrugged his shoulders and listened.

Five

Kim and Ralph sat, waiting their turn to address the Board of Directors of the Wild River Casinos Corporation. They both felt well prepared, yet a little tense. After all, they were proposing an unusual name, one for which they might catch some serious flak from the stodgy receptacles of conventional culture who spread their posteriors on capacious, upholstered chairs before them, on the dais from which they deliberated and pontificated.

It was a marvel to watch them operate. One had a shiny pate sparkling through a dingy tonsure of fringe gray. Another fiddled with a long cigar, which he could not smoke in the non-smoking paneled boardroom. Yet a third seemed abstracted from the meeting, stolidly going through the motions of being a director. At least that was the observation of Kim, who, as a thorough liberal, disliked the cake of custom that held the all-male dork conservative panel in place.

Anne Stole, an acquaintance to both Kim and Ralph, sat down beside them, extracting a cigarette from a silver case, but not lighting it. She rolled it between her thumb and forefinger, almost like a nervous tic. It was not a tic, however, but her way of resisting the nicotine habit that had darkened her life for over 20 years. The seemingly eccentric behavior was her substitute for Nicodent. It had been working for over a year, this curious mode of abstinence, with the exception of a solitary cigarette on New Year's Eve, when she was drunk and festive.

Ralph peered sideways at Anne. "How's it going?" he asked friendlily.

"I'm here for the fireworks," she returned. "Jim, down at city hall, just told me what you're gonna do."

"It's a great name!" enthused Kim, who was so pleased no one was smoking in the room. After all, this place of the higher corporate decision-making was officially a no-smoking venue. Not that that guaranteed the intended results at other health-oriented facilities around town. "Long Dark River Casino is more than a name!" she burbled. "It is creative; it is pure literature."

Ralph smiled. "We added Otherness."

Kim cracked a smile. "And Avocet," she added.

Anne's eyes reflected the ceiling lights as she summed the words. "The Long Dark River, Otherness, and Avocet Casino." She paused. "What an awesome name for a casino!"

"We think so," said Kim airily. "It's sort of brilliant, doncha think?"

Anne nodded, and Ralph smiled with his eyes.

The meeting was gaveled to order by Justin Claymore, the chair of Wild River Casinos, Inc. He was the one who had a shiny pate sparkling through a dingy tonsure of very thin gray. "I call this meeting to order," he announced somberly, though with an undertone of the peremptory.

Messieurs Wausewski and Pryor, the remainder of the triumvirate at the dais, visibly settled in for another evening meeting in the spotlight, perhaps a trying session. Wausewski was the one with the long cigar which he could not smoke. Pryor was the abstracted one, the closest to a visionary or intellectual that Wild River Casinos had in its employ. His eyes seem to focus in the middle to far distance whereas Wausewski's seemed to find focus on the roundness of his cigar, as though he were most willfully fending off a nicotine fit.

Anne ramped up the rate at which she twirled her unlit cigarette in her hand. She felt sexually attracted to the dreamer, the one without a cigar before her, above her, the one that still had a full head of hair, looking down on her, as though he might want to….

Justin Claymore went through several agenda items, routine stuff, except the appointment of a new business manager for one of the casinos in western Illinois. Of the 30 or so people in attendance, it seemed there would be no dissent from the appointment until, at the very last moment, a young man in bright summerweight checked shirt, who said he was a stockholder, stood up abruptly, raising his hand. He said he wanted to see the résumé and references of the new hire, to make sure the new employee was what he said he was. "I do not want to lose money because we hire a felon or something," he snarled. "Lemme see his application!"

Claymore smiled unctuously at the young man. "We will be happy to give you a look at his credentials. But we can only do that in the main office. They will let you take a look there. They'll let you see them in a secure cubicle. You can't take it out of the office."

Though he was clearly not completely satisfied with Claymore's response, the young man desisted from challenging Claymore. He said he would visit the office if Claymore and the others would make sure he got quick and easy access to the file. And to that all of them assented affably.

"Now, to the next item on the agenda," monotoned Claymore. He peered down, adjusting his bifocals, pausing, his eyes searching. "It is, of course, to invite nominations for the name of the new casino we are building here in Quinlan. Does anyone have a name to submit?"

Before Kim or Ralph could raise a hand, the young man again shot his hand up. "I have a name," he guffawed. "How about the Felonious Filch or Aggravated Assault…"

Claymore banged his gavel. "Out of order! Out of order!"

"Or The River Leech," continued the man. "Or…"

Long Dark River Casino

"Out of order! You will have to leave now! Or do we need to have Officer Burke over there escort you out?" Claymore extended his hand toward the uniformed officer on duty.

The young man grumbled, "I'm outta here. This place is for neo-Nazis only!" And he marched briskly out, his eyes hooded, in a very dark huff.

"Now let us resume," said Claymore calmly. "We would be happy to entertain some serious nominations for a name for the casino, one that will preferably help to draw in gamblers by the droves."

Wausewski touched Claymore's shoulder to get his attention and then stage-whispered into his ear, prompting Claymore to correct himself. "They are our visitors," he grinned wryly, "visitors with entertainment dollars to spend. They are not gamblers. They are, indeed, our guests, our honored guests."

Ralph felt a surge of disgust at the treacly euphemism for "mark" or "sucker" but he kept his own counsel. He raised his hand. "I have a suggestion."

Claymore nodded, pointing at him. "Fire when ready, Gridley."

"I propose you name the new casino the Long Dark River Casino."

Kim side-glanced approvingly at Ralph. She felt he had condensed the name most aptly.

Six

Professor Gary Klemetson was out birdwatching, where he was most truly in his element, the Quinlan Nature Conservancy, a 400-acre preserve, privately owned by the Eastern Iowa Friends of the Prairie. That organization was the love of his life, rivaled only by his affection for his pet cockatoo, Rigoletto. He had given much time, money, sweat, and consternation to the Friends of the Prairie. In fact, he had served as President for two terms as well as endowing it with a substantial fund for protecting and expanding habitat for raptors (not to mention his monthly "tithe" to the green organizational object of his affections). He loved it; he loved the earth; he loved all feathered things that flew, especially raptors, and most especially red-tailed hawks. For him the red-tailed exhibited the most beauty and true athletic prowess—its swooping flight and determined diving were awesome!—as well as the most spirituality—yes, spirituality—of all the raptors.

Prof G looked for the red-tailed hawk constantly on his birding outings. It was always a thrill that entailed his going, at least in his mind's eye, onto a different, better plane of existence. The bird was good medicine that connected him to the spirit world! He had brought the hawk into his life as a guest of the Anishnabeg tribe when he became a pipe-bearer on a sabbatical he took on the White Earth Reservation in northern Minnesota...

Seven

Out on Anishnabeg, aka Chippewa, aka Ojibway land over five years ago, on a bright November day, Prof Gary had sighted a sky full of red-tailed hawks, maybe 40 in all, kettling above him, as if shape-shifting a message to him. He felt in his bones the approach of something spiritual, but he could not put his finger on it, at least not until the hawks finished their desultory, frenzied flight overhead. They seemed to cavort and play a kind of tag for over an hour before they made their descent. All of a sudden, they broke ranks and circled down to perches on limbs of trees. Their energy throbbed in the cerulean blue and their silhouettes seemed like shadows on high. This connected with his heart and soul, a "peak experience" in Maslowian terms that was to soon become palpably more intense.

The hawks fanned out over a wide swath of land, most out of his line of sight or descending too far removed from where he stood to be seen, by naked eye or through the field binoculars he held raptly to his eyes. But one solitary hawk circled almost directly over him, finding a nearby tree to land on. It was if the bird were dropping by for a visit to have a chat!

His Anishnabeg friend Blue Kettle nudged his arm. "The hawk is here for us, friend."

"Ahhh," intoned Prof G, excited but bemused. He iterated simply under his breath, "Here for us. Here for us."

"Look!" said Blue Kettle animatedly. "The hawk flies closer!"

With unparalleled grace and vibrant with natural power, the hawk swooped to another perch not more than twenty feet away in an osage orange, one of the trees that formed a windbreak on Blue Kettle's property, home to his auto repair shop.

A sound of words Prof Gary could not understand broke the silent canopy of the tree. "I am your grandmother, Red Feather," spoke the hawk. "Do you not recognize me?"

A great sense of gravity enveloped the features of Blue Kettle, for he was summarily awestruck. He was silent for a long time before he spoke hesitantly, in a faltering voice. "I do know you grandma Red Feather." He waved an arm toward Dr. G, "And I have brought my professor friend to honor you!"

Prof G grinned thinly. "Sociologist and anthropologist, researcher of tribal culture and authenticator of enrolled member status, at your service."

"He is our honorary peace pipe bearer, Red Feather. He is a white man who walks in our moccasins."

"I feel his strength. He is not like the bad whites of Minnesota who hanged the 38 Lakota at Fort Mankato in 1862. He comes from somewhere else. Where?"

"Iowa."

Prof G grinned. "On the Mississippi River, from Quinlan, a rivertown where I work at Quinlan University."

"He teaches there," added Blue Kettle.

"He is of a feather with us," said Red Feather in a ghost-like voice now, sounding most scary to Prof G who was kind of getting the willies listening to an Anishnabeg ghost-hawk speaking in English. He fully knew the Anishnabeg were a very spiritual people. But this was beyond the pale, a "civilized" ghost-hawk who communicated in English. He must take all this down on paper as soon as it was over! He should be able to get at least a short article into **Spiritual Anthropology**, one of his favorite journals. They hadn't heard from him for quite a while, and he could use the publishing credit to help justify his sabbatical, where what he was doing could best be described as passively imbibing aboriginal culture in a cool post-modern poseur way.

"Blue Kettle," the hawk said in its eery tone from its aerie in the osage, "You must do something for me."

"What is it? Anything, Red Feather. I will do anything for you."

"You must soon fix your friend's old Chevy and ride back to Iowa with him. You will have a vision because of this."

At this, the hawk flew, riding the warm air into a circling pattern overhead. Prof G and Blue Kettle peered upward, hands shielding their eyes against the intense sun, until the ghost-hawk disappeared in the distance. Both were totally wrapped in the event, too absorbed for words, struck speechless by what they had just beheld.

They were looking at a long trip back to Iowa, one that promised to become an Anishnabeg vision quest.

EIGHT

Ralph and Kim wanted to visit the Meskwaki tribal casino near Tama, Iowa, to see what they could learn of the competition. As business people, particularly as marketers, they had learned in their business courses that getting a feel for the opposing brand or brands could lead to good things, usually—like life itself—unexpected things. So, they drove for a leisurely afternoon of gaming via Highway 30—the old "Lincoln Highway" graced by its copious historic markers and mileposts—through the recently flooded-out, though now much rehabbed large city (by Iowa standards) of Cedar Rapids. This is what Professor G would call participant observation, thought Ralph. For me and Kim, it is marketing research. Somehow he felt smug and self-satisfied with that thought, almost as if it were a way to challenge the craggy, if not flaky, intellectual pre-eminence of Dr. G.

Long Dark River Casino

As they navigated their way through the historic Czech Village of downtown Cedar Rapids, flanking the now tranquil Cedar River which had inflicted a 500-year flood on the city, slightly less than a year earlier, Kim enthused, "Why don't we stop and see Barb? We can see how she's doing after the flood!"

Ralph nodded his agreement. "We both know where she works," he said, as he swung right toward the Bohemian Café.

"She's the one who still likes s'mores, even after graduating from Quinlan. She's still a teen at heart, at least a part of her." Kim pointed, directing Ralph to take the next turn. "She even likes that young singer who's reviving Tony Bennett songs."

"She is a throwback, eh? She likes that guy from Canada who mimics 'I Lost My Heart In San Francisco.' What's his name?"

"Michael Bublé. He's from Vancouver, and he's done well in the States. He did a concert in the Quad Cities that Barb loved."

Ralph shrugged as he wheeled around a corner toward the café. "I appreciate her nostalgia for the oldies. Punk rock and hip-hop turn me off, though I tolerate hip-hop much better than punk. Must be those Donald Goines' 'ghetto realism' novels I read, especially **Cool Daddy** and **Dope Fiend**."

Kim felt her secret love for Ralph grow just a little more as he slant-parked directly in front of the Bohemian Café. She could see Barb waitressing behind the plate glass storefront, emblazoned in Gothic gilt letters with the name of the café. Though Barb owned the café, putting to good applied use her B.A. in Business Administration, she regularly served customers both to enhance the enterprise's bottom line as well as keep in touch with the customer as a genuine, 3-D person, not an avatar, something that even great successes such as Starbucks had lost sight of recently (to the detriment of their balance sheet).

"We gotta test market the new casino name on Barb," said Ralph, as they uncoiled themselves from his Toyota sedan. "Barb will tell us straightaway what she thinks!"

Kim mimicked, "We gotta test market the name" under her breath, as she stretched tall, getting out the kinks after their two-hour drive from Quinlan. The old historic Lincoln Highway had offered her resplendent views of silos, fields, farm houses, bathed in the purest golden sunshine of a torrid August day where she felt she could hear the corn growing were it not for the steady thrum of Ralph's car. The sun and the historic route had burnished the beauty of the Iowa scenes passing by the passenger-side window. Even the kestrels and red-tailed hawks had an immanence about them that was jaw-dropping.

Barb had seen them coming and was soon at the doorway of her eatery, her hands folded over a tricolor Bohemian-patterned apron and a gingham dress. She wore a calico sunbonnet. The outfit made little sense to Kim, who guessed it was a kind of jerry-rigged get-up, constrained by what the floods had swept away and made possible by what could be purchased locally as replacement fabric. She dared not ask, for fear of twerking off Barb.

Barb smiled broadly and ushered them into the inner confines of her eatery. Framed pictures of historic sights around town were lined up in phalanxes on the wall. Yet, there were no pictures at all of the flood. As Ralph surveyed the walls, he observed, "I thought for sure you'd have some photos of the devastation up. It's been almost a year since it happened."

Barb nodded, her forehead slightly furrowed. "You are very observant," she noted, her eyes lit up, her body suffused with a tensile muscular energy. She twirled on a heel, her gaze transiting over all the framed photos, some of them reproductions of daguerreotypes taken by a regionally famed photographer of the 1870s to the turn of the century, Caleb V. Farr. "See those over there," she pointed. "Those are Farrs."

"Like far-out," quipped Ralph. "Or just Farr."

"No, Farrs," corrected Barb. "The plural. These are photos that Cedar Rapids' own Caleb Carr took over a century ago."

"Pretty impressive," observed Kim, half-believing what she said, and half-saying what she felt Barb wanted to hear. "They sure make Cedar Rapids look like an inviting place to live." She usually was tired after any substantial road trip, but this afternoon she was not. Perhaps some subtle change in her circadian rhythms brought on by a minor hormone imbalance. Probably nothing, but definitely rather quirky.

"They are very impressive!" chimed in Ralph. "Very impressive indeed!"

To this Barb resonated, "I love this town. I grew up here and now I'm back. I had offers at several companies after I got my B.A. in Business. But this is where I am happy, running this business."

"You gotta do what makes you happy!" echoed Kim.

"Yes," said Barb simply, her voice changing to a confidential tone. "How may I help you? You said something on the phone about my old professor, Gary Klemetson?"

"Yes, Prof G. We want to talk about him," said Ralph.

Kim followed, "We have heard rumors, especially from Jim the Janitor at Quinlan City Hall that the Professor possesses the powers of an Ojibway medicine man."

Ralph paused meaningfully. "In fact, we think he may be an outright Ojibway shaman. That's how good he might be!"

Barb unwound her hands that had been entwined in her apron. "Yes, I have heard stuff like that, too. Been hearing it for years. He liked to promote himself as that, too, in the gen ed class I took from him, Anthro 101, Intro to Cultural Anthropology. But I never took it seriously. I thought he was just sexually frustrated or something, that he needed an outlet through his imagination." She stopped and gazed at Kim, then Ralph. "Should I have taken him seriously?"

Long Dark River Casino

A customer came in and Barb escorted him to a table near the back of the café, then returned to repeat, "Should I?" A certain nervousness emerged in her voice that was not present at the first iteration of the question.

"We don't know," said Ralph in a businesslike monotone. "That's what we're here for."

"And why are you so interested in Prof G?" Barb asked. "He seems harmless enough. How can a bookworm and a birdwatcher ever be a problem?"

"We aren't accusing him of being a problem," riposted Kim. "We're just interested in knowing about those famously rumored powers of his."

"Why?"

"We have our reasons."

"That's schoolyard talk. But I'll excuse it for now, cuz you are my friends and I don't mind sharing with friends, even if I don't know their motivation." Barb retreated a few feet and sat down heavily at an unoccupied table, inviting with a slow flourish of her arm for Ralph and Kim to join her.

They huddled at the rustic homemade Czech-style wooden table, a small pot containing an African violet punctuating the center of the shagbark hickory table, flanked by caddies of dairy creamer and sugar, in individual, handy baby-blue packets. A late-summer heavyset bluebottle fly buzzed in the slight breeze created by the overhead fan, so labored that he threatened to fall out of the air.

Barb placed her hands palms-down on the table surface. "Let me tell you about Prof G, the white Indian."

The buzzing insect has asthma, thought Kim.

And as she listened to Barb, the bluebottle's circling flight reminded her of the flight pattern of a red-tailed hawk.

But for some reason, neither Ralph nor she remembered to ask her about the Long Dark River Casino…

NINE

Prof G and his Ojibway friend Blue Kettle were at that very moment busy in pursuit of a vision quest, far up in northern Minnesota, on the White Earth Reservation. They had tried to get Winona LaDuke, the famous Ojibway activist and politician, to hike into the woods with them. As an environmentalist, they felt she might appreciate coming along. But she had been too busy on the phone with Ralph Nader, whose vice presidential running mate she had been for one of his long-shot runs at the White House. Blue Kettle had simply said sotto voce and elliptically, "She can sometime get that way." What that meant, Prof G could only hazard a guess. Whatever it was, it had to be something ugly, provoked by that damn Nader. That guy made bad things happen; he could bring out the darkside manitous with great regularity, and let them inadvertently loose on you without even a hint of trying to do so. It was downright awesome how Nader fit into the scheme of things!

The two would-be Vision Questers trudged into the Minnesota woods, deeper and deeper into the stands of birch and aspen. Redwinged blackbirds cawed from perches near concavities featuring marshes and cattails, adding an eerie C-flat counterpoint to the march of the conjuring duo. As they got deeper into the woods, deer flies began to attack, and poison ivy began showing up on the narrow pathways. Slapping at the deerflies, occasionally finding his hand cupping a mishmash glistening with his own blood, as telltale shiny "leaves of three" brushed his lower arms and legs, was more than enough to dissuade Prof G from any early-onset visions. Blue Kettle is used to this, he thought. Perhaps he doesn't need calamine lotion and an O-positive blood transfusion to integrate harmoniously into the natural world. But I, child of a more comfortable environmentalism—the more affluent might call it Volvo Environmentalism avec chardonnay and brie—am not equipped, physically or temperamentally, to suffer this.

Prof G slapped at the back of his neck. Another bloody mess, most of it his blood, appeared in his hand. He began to feel nauseous, like he might projectile vomit or something else gross. Vision Quest! he thought, his jaw set in a determined line. Minny miney Manitou, wouldn't you, voulez-vous?

Finally, after a couple miles of trudging, Prof G asked, "How much further, Blue Kettle?" He wanted a drink of water in the worst way.

"Not far," monotoned Blue Kettle. He paused. "And you don't get any water. Thirst helps you get a vision."

Prof G felt his mind tumbling into a deep ravine of depression. Dark thoughts rode into his frontal cortex, cantering horseshit all over his synapses, spilling Minnesota merde onto his hippocampus. How was he to achieve a vision, The Vision, out of this beshatting of his precious, inimitable brain? "I need a drink of water," he growled. "I feel dehydrated and---"

Blue Kettle cut him off. "That's the idea! When you are about to faint, you might get your vision then. That's the point! To suffer in the wilderness is to see better."

"What if I just faint?"

"If you do, I'll wake you up. But only after I have had my vision," Blue Kettle chuckled. "I wouldn't want you to interfere with good shaman's work!"

"Interfere? Like I'm just a tourist or something."

Blue Kettle nodded. "That's a good word for you: tourist."

"I prefer ethnographer," retorted Prof G testily. "That's a kind of anthropologist, if you don't know!"

Blue Kettle backhanded a rivulet of sweat off his forehead. "I know anthropologist. I know ethnographer. We have had many such people visit the White Earth Reservation in my time. Many. All on grant money of some kind."

"But I am different!" contested the Professor. "I am here on my own money, out of love for your culture, and the promise it holds of enabling me to have better insights. To wit, here today, this pristine, sultry afternoon, I seek a vision with you."

Blue Kettle spit out a long stream of tobacco juice. "My patootie!" he exclaimed, not in Algonquin.

Prof G knew what patootie meant, and it was not an Algonquin word. So, he simply kept his own counsel for the moment as they trudged further into the seemingly infinite birch, aspen, and tamarack trees. He thought "quest" was just the right word for his long march into misery. Hell, he could get more of a vision staying at home surfing his pc!

Suddenly, Blue Kettle halted at the opening of a meadow verdant with late summer flowers, their whites, reds, and blues stippling the lush greenness. Asters, wild honeysuckle, buttercups, and goldenrod dazzled the verdant tapestry and accented the warm summer air with sharp, pleasing scents. Prof G could tell that Blue Kettle was more alert, his carriage more rigid, as he looked beyond the meadow. For what? He could not see anything remarkable, worth looking for—just more trees and bushes, all too compactly dense for his druthers. He could feel his skin itch already. Or was his mind getting psychosomatic on him? Indeed, he could prophecy a true vision now: He could see himself now dying of a severe case of poison ivy! His pallid, unaboriginal skin lacked the immunity of his Ojibway companion who, incidentally, had become most difficult just immediately of late!

Blue Kettle squinted into the oblique rays of the sun enveloping the meadow. "It is the Midewiwin. Do you hear the drum?"

"I see nothing," muttered miserable Prof G. "But I think I hear something."

"It is the Midewiwin drum," informed Blue Kettle. "It calls us."

Like, yeah, it beckons us, thought the Prof. To a hell. Midewiwin must be Algonquin for poison ivy-and-dehydration hell! He fell onto the meadow grass like a rock and began to chew voraciously at the bunched grass and inviting wildflowers, eager to imbibe whatever moisture he could from the expansive verdure and its blades and blossoms. He made suckling noises, his lips fastened to a splay of grass, causing Blue Kettle to bridle, at the unmanliness of any man, even a white man, behaving in such a sniveling, disgusting fashion. For a culture that prided itself on manly courage and bravery in the face of overwhelmingly unpromising odds, the sight of the professor groveling before him, eating grass of all things, really reinforced his negative stereotype of whites! Grass-eaters! Bad medicine!

The drum somewhere ahead continued to throb. Prof G got up and labored on behind Blue Kettle. The tympanic beat grew louder as they moved on, almost, it seemed to the Prof, to the cadence of their moccasin-padded feet. The rhythm helped to subdue his fears and nausea. Perhaps there was something to the power of a drum that inculcated harmony. It was even better than a certain bassist's effect on him back in Quinlan, where the rock group "Quinlan Quota" played occasionally at the Mississippi Mellow Club. He took the band in whenever he could, and found they soothed the nerves of academe better than anything else, even the dirty martinis he was so fond of.(Prof G thought of martinis as a bearer of heightened consciousness, comparable to another kind of vision that fasting and suffering in the wilderness could also produce.)

Blue Kettle waved him on each time he lagged, famished and dehydrated. He was becoming tired enough and battered enough for a vision anytime. The drum drew them on, until a lodge emerged into distinct definition in a man-axed clearing in the deep birch and aspen. "It is the Midewiwin Lodge," whispered Blue Kettle. "It is important that we speak softly from now on. We do not want to anger the manitous."

Prof G nodded like a metronome, almost too tired to care. He could stand to stop arguing, too. When your conscious mind almost flatlines, maybe that means you're on the verge of a true vision. If so, he felt he had amply deserved any vision he got.

The curved features of the lodge greeted them around a bend in the path. For all the hype Blue Kettle had built up, it was a letdown, a primitive structure of bent birch, open to the sky through the latticework. He could now discern that there were a good dozen Ojibway seated on the floor of the lodge, half of them facing the other half, each with his knees drawn up, appearing most solemn through hooded eyes. For an ethnographer, things were beginning to look most promis-

Long Dark River Casino

ing! He could already see his name gracing the table of contents of a new issue of **Spiritual Anthropology.**

As they approached, the drummer, beating fervently on a drum consisting of deerhide drawn taut over a hollowed-out stump, accelerated his tempo, his hands flashing in a flurry of Mide ecstasy. The Midewiwin Society assembled behind him began to chant in Algonquin, their eyes seemingly unaware of the advancing pair. They were voicing their very beings, trying to connect with the manitous that were abundant, yet normally not seen. They were trying to do what the Ojibway had done over the millennia—abide in harmony with spirits, good and evil, so that they might live successfully in their tribal ways, appeasing nature in order to do so.

The chant went on and the drum beat on, unfazed by Prof G and Blue Kettle. The power of the Midewiwin exerted itself profoundly. Prof G observed that the birds had ceased singing, a rare event indeed! A profound peace and somnolence descended upon the Ojibway. The birds had tuned into this tranquility, ceasing producing C-sharps from their perches in trees and bushes. The Everywhere Being was immanent.

The Midewiwin was a profound expression of the tribe's unity on a lofty spiritual plane. The Ojibway expressed themselves at their best this way. Only the Sun Dance of the Lakota rivaled this ceremony. The individual was submerged in the group and thereby enhanced. The individual Indian, a frail red bag of bone and blood, insignificant in its mass and bulk, became one with the Everywhere Being through the manitous. At least the good manitous. One of their number, the windingo, was a very evil spirit-being and was devoutly to be avoided. If a member of the tribe died, everyone avoided speaking that person's name, camouflaging the lodge where he had lived and the one where you now live, for not to protect yourself was to invite an attack by the windingo, a most destructive creature. Every Ojibway knew the bad side of a departed member of the tribe could return to haunt you through the windingo!

The shaman, Old Elk, stood behind the drummer and near the degree pole, that separated him from the Midewiwin Society. He had become a shaman as a young man when he had contracted tuberculosis. He would have died if the spirit world had not cured him. Through the ordeal, the power to communicate with the manitous had been bestowed on him. For decades, he had been able to connect his tribe with the forces of nature that lay behind every creek, rock, tree, animal, lake, and mountain. All that is, is spiritual. He had developed a reputation as a shaman with great powers, and he accepted that as true, for he had not chosen the role of shaman; it had chosen him. So he was pleased to shake the rattle in his right hand, calling the manitou, as he held strips of snakeskin in his left. He savored his role as shaman as he went among the members of the Midewiwin Society, handing each a medicine stick. He relished the role as he lit pine needles in the glowing coals of the sacred fire and applied a flashing flame to the sacred tobacco leaves nestled in a birch tray (a tray that his sister, Eyes Running, had crafted for him last autumn). At first the tobacco resisted the flame, failing to catch fire. But then it began to smolder and burn.

Old Elk set the rattle down on the moose skin on which he had arrayed the tools of his spiritual trade, including a pipe of catlinite and a collection of snakeskins, the dessicated mortal coils of a selection of most everything that slithered in Ojibway land. For the snake was special in its import and effects on the Midewiwin during the healing ceremony in which he invoked the manitous and their powers. The snakeskins, along with the rattle and tobacco, whose smoke he wafted with an eagle feather over a sick ten-year-old boy, lying limply, near death, before him, were central to the sacred ceremony.

Old Elk placed the snake skins on the boy's body. He arrayed them in a geometric pattern on his chest, crossing them to achieve a starburst effect. The remaining skins he laid out along the child's legs and arms. A final one, he draped on his forehead. And thus began the Midewiwin, the healing ceremony.

Prof G looked on raptly. Blue Kettle had participated many times, but stood aloof, feeling constrained by the Prof's presence. This was strange as the Prof had long been a friend of the tribe, not only doing research on the White Earth Reservation, but also pitching in to rehab rundown houses inhabited by Anishnabeg. They had even been what one could call friends, for several years anyway, keeping in touch by letters, phone calls, and e-mails. Yet, in the face of the sacred healing ceremony, a distance set in between them that underscored the depth of the rift between the White Earth Rez and the White Man.

Prof G and Blue Kettle exchanged glances. It was as if they had just met, not knowing what step to take next. Invite the white into the ritual? It hardly seemed appropriate today, though the Professor had participated before, even published a monograph on the Midewiwin.

A red-winged blackbird called, swaying in the breeze atop a spindly alder tree. In the lodge, the boy had responded to the snake skins and the "sucking cure," administered as the skins were pulled off. He opened his eyes, his expression blank.

"The red-wing is a spirit-being," intoned the Prof-as-scholar. "The bird has heard the rattle. It has been sent by a manitou. It has brought good medicine to the boy."

Slowly, the boy sat up from his lying-down position, his back erect. He was fervently blinking his eyes in opposition to his blank expression, eyes dull and unfocussed, now dimmed, slowly becoming brighter.

Then, suddenly, a small image appeared on his forehead. The Red Hawk. The boy fell dead to the earthen lodge floor.

The assembled Midewiwin Society turned accusatory stares at Prof G.

Ten

Ralph parked his venerable, rust-fissured-and-fringed Toyota steed some six spaces down from the twin aluminum-and-plate-glass entry doors to the Meskwaki tribal headquarters. Kim peered at the robin-egg-blue sky and exclaimed, "What a great day!" Her sentiment would prove a tad premature.

Their friend, Sam Sixkiller, strode forth from the modern-looking building, smiling, his hand extended. Both Kim and Ralph shook his hand. Kim thought: For a traditionalist, he—anomalously—would likely do a good job of marketing for any Big Board company. Then, she checked her thoughts. Of course, he would! Though not Big Board, the Meskwaki Casino was an enterprise he promoted to one and all ceaselessly. It was the inamorata of his life, mostly because he could deploy substantial revenue to the Meskwaki cultural center and museum. These institutions betokened the resuscitation of the Red Earth people's time-honored traditions. Sam'd be damn good at marketing pizza, soft drinks, pc's, or Quinlan University. It just so happened his product was gaming.

"Welcome to Meskwaki land!" enthused Sam Sixkiller. "I'm more happy to see you than the likes of Jonathan Sleeping Horse," he added darkly.

Always Sleeping Horse, his great nemesis, came quickly to the fore in any encounter, even if he had to adventitiously interject him. Sam suffered from an obsession with Sleeping Horse, the man he'd focused all his pure hatred of the Meskwaki progressives on, those traitors who had been selling out their culture ever since their hereditary monarch had been deposed by a two-vote margin in 1937. He especially loathed the 1934 legislation, the Indian Reorganization Act, that enabled such Western concepts as "government" to be imposed on his tribe.

Kim and Ralph knew all this well. Grounded in their knowledge, they recognized that Sam was complex. And because he was complex, there were parts of him that had proved most helpful.

A couple Meskwaki youngsters, munching Dove Bars, appeared behind Sam. "These are my grandsons," he beamed. "Sonny Sixkiller is the tough one in the red shirt. Billy is in the blue shirt. Both are fine boys."

Tough seemed not an apt term as both seven-year-olds shrunk behind Sam's hulking bulk. (Sam liked to regularly indulge in the buffet at the casino and it showed in his obesity, the roll of fat that surged over his belt, bearing beadwork of traditional Meskwaki designs and artwork. And the word "CASINO" ran across his beaded girth to proclaim his favorite product and cause.)

Kim pointed to his belt. "The Long Dark River Casino can use your help." She paused, appending, "We can use your help."

Sam bridled inwardly. He had grave reservations about helping a rival casino, but he knew he had to. A Red Hawk had spoken to him in his dreams for months. That hawk was a manitou, the last hereditary chief of the tribe, counseling him to assist the couple from Quinlan. He would never sleep well again unless he did so. His ancestors would see to that!

Eleven

Jim the Janitor, Ph.D. manqué, Quinlan University quondam adjunct, stood before his Iowa History night class, trying to get his next word out. He suffered from Tourette's Syndrome, a rare disease that leaves you unable to control blurting out dirty words while experiencing stress. "Does…" He paused. "Does everyone have the freaking assignment done?" he asked. Usually, after he got warmed up, his words flowed fairly well, on prepared material, at least. It was on the off-the-cuff stuff that the Tourette's could kick in, prompting him to say something inappropriate or off-color. It was during such interludes that his puling career as an adjunct became most at risk. By way of taking care, he often told himself: You cannot let any old word fly and expect your career to survive the classroom, Tourette's or no. Think of all the years earning a Ph.D., including two years of dissertation research in Paris. For a few compulsive wicked words, to waste that?

Unfortunately, Tourette's is not, like maladies everywhere, an affliction you can control at will. (Otherwise, there would be no serious illnesses at all!) Consequently, Jim had to regularly explain comments that students complained about or had grown juicy on the grapevines of the University. The QU administration had gone through several rounds with him, and because he presented his problem in a sincere, humble way, they had become sympathetic, even a defender, citing the Americans with Disabilities Act in his defense. Accordingly, Jim had achieved a personal record, surviving an entire five semesters (one course per term) at QU. Previously, his Tourette's had gotten him fired at two community colleges after but one semester. (Quinlan County Community College had wanted to fire him after the first week, but accepted his alleged disability enough for him to complete his course in European History, albeit with a few more unbidden expletives.) Tourette's, he'd found, is very hard for colleges to find credible. Even the psychological profiles he'd provided from the University of Iowa Hospitals they seemed to find suspect. How can one curse in the most appalling terms straight out of the blue while discussing the Swedish King Gustavus Adolphus at the Battle of Lutzen in 1632? It struck some college administrators as more a moral defect than a medical condition.

Twelve

Professor Gary strolled into the gleaming confines of the Quinlan Mall, the dominating and proud commercial centerpiece of Quinlan, Iowa, a town of almost 30,000 hardy, cornpone-eating souls, located on the left bank of the Mississippi River. He was looking for a security outlet for his home computer. He had been having a flummoxing, myriad of problems of late keeping that steed of a personal computer he called "Valhalla" on the right and true digital path, for a variety of reasons he had been sorting out lately. One little nettling issue after another he had resolved, to come down to this: the plug-in for the wall socket. Maybe the grounded three-prong male device he had purchased at the university bookstore did not fit so well with the female outlet. Prof Gary chortled inwardly. Even the thought of electrical devices metaphorically simulating sex made him blush. He was a blusher alright on matters sexual, and that went way back in his life, beginning with the dawning of his sexuality. As he wound down his career in the gloried ivied halls of Quinlan U, he realized his sexuality, in his mid-sixties, was pretty much a glint off his hormone-addled teens, dimmed for sure, but definitely a veracious verisimilitude of the young Gary on a star-struck summer night under the fig trees of Oroville, California, his hometown.

Prof Gary felt a surge of personal, psychic energy charge through his 64-year-old body as he walked across the sparkling mauve-and-crimson, patterned tile that spanned the vast lobby-cum-atrium of the illustrious Quinlan Mall, a consumer mecca toward which devotees of glittering, quality products, cleverly planned for obsolescence, and chemical concoctions, euphemistically termed "fast food," came by the droves. None of this—or at least not much of it, and only as necessary—was for him. He had long imbibed only unprocessed, natural foods, plant edibles that had been nurtured solely by sun, water, and soil. For he was a vegetarian, highly averse to factory food that spewed out of extruding machines exactly as plastic parts did. (In fact, if one factored in the plastic dishware for frozen meals, the analogy would not be exactly apt, because the plastic itself had long ago—beginning with Bird's Eye—become integral to the mass synthetic national food experience.) The true cruciferous crudités and other non-polluting variants of comestibles that comprised his culinary forte had led him to a sturdy age 64 and would likely lead him further up the actuarial table, beyond both the median and mean for those of his demographic status, which is to say "mixed race." (Prof Gary was one of those more unusual blood mixes on the American continent: Norwegian, province of Nord-Trondelag, forcibly injected into the Wintu tribe of Northern California at the behest and passion of the earliest wave of 49ers seeking their fortune.)

Prof Gary owed his demographic niche status to his great-great grandfather, Olaf, who had emigrated from Norway in search of a better life. He hailed from near Trondheim, where he had faced the futility of trying to make a living on so-called "farmland" that slanted toward a fjord a thousand feet below at a breathtakingly, scary angle. Olaf could not make a living on the five hectares he had inherited by primogeniture laws then current in the region of Norway, then part of a condominium dominated by Sweden, that would become in 1905 a newly minted nation, Norway. And since Olaf, at age 20, could in no way afford a boat for the more promising life of a cod fisherman, and since he was unmarried, both for want of economic prospects for himself and the sparse availability of nubile young women in Sundnes village, he decided to emigrate to "Amerika." Olaf's father, Tellef Klemetson—Prof Gary's great-great-great grandfather—had been receiving a steady stream of letters from his nephew, Gunnar, who had departed almost two years earlier for the Minnesota Territory. Gunnar wrote glowingly of the good rich prairie soil in a combination of broken English and good Norwegian, all in the florid orthog-

Long Dark River Casino

raphy he had learned in the Sundnes school from Miss Kjersti Klemetson, one of his aunts, the unmarried one who could stay teaching as long as she remained single, and that was pretty much a lead-pipe cinch for a woman of 32 with an off-putting personality in a village of 115, the annual count taken at the center of community life, the St. Olaf stave church, as of the year 1849. All these factors, and more—not least of which was that it had become legal to emigrate from Norway in the 1840s—informed his profoundly wrenching decision to leave his homeland and family. This was, as demographers term it, a decision prompted largely by "push factors" over "pull factors." Gold would have never beckoned enough in the Mexican state of California to draw him out of virtually medieval Norway had it not been for his extreme, absolute poverty. For one "push," absolute poverty in the Norway of 1849 meant scurvy from a poor winter diet, that the villagers corrected by gorging on the efflorescence of wildflowers in the spring.

Such was the **Cliff's Notes** version of Prof Gary's own curious genealogy (omitting how he happened to move from California to Iowa, about which maybe something tasteful later) as he strode purposely toward the Electric Shack on the far side of the mall to buy an adapter for a 110-volt home office outlet. He was thinking of the California Gold Rush as a contemporary fact. His was a psychology that not even the cantilevered, multi-storied, futuristic Quinlan Mall could detract from far backward-looking nostalgia.

The Quinlan Mall was far from crowded on a Thursday evening. Yet Prof Gary could see a scattering of shoppers and window shoppers. It was, he thought, a good time for a mixed-race Viking-Wintu to visit the great mall. The off-hour meant a modest agglomeration of people would be available for him to observe, the abiding calling of a Ph.D. sociologist; yet, there would not be so many of the critters that he had to weave his way through them as a kind of mall cowboy, warding off consumer stampedes headed for some sacred-secular "Quinlan blue light special" somewhere in the four-story canyons of Iowa's greatest mall. For he knew, that consumers, like cattle, were highly suggestible. On this fundamental marketing "truth" rested the prosperity of the United States.

Prof Gary worked his way along the first-tier concourse, glancing at shops as he went, and stopping briefly to window-shop at one. The big sales were on. He had in mind a new tie, for the first time in years. Some of his colleagues, and even more of the students, had begun to complain about the lack of variety in his wardrobe, suggesting acidly that Quinlan University had perhaps garnisheed his checks on court order to pay off some outstanding, long-overdue debt. But that was far from true. The truth was that he was a lifelong bachelor who lived amid a chaos of books and computers and file cabinets and that the grace note of a tie would never occur to him. He was more interested in his psyche and mind, the depths of his being—not the patina of life and its glitzy superficialities. But the

Long Dark River Casino

biting criticism had been forcefully made from a number of quarters over a protracted length of time and its acerbity had finally registered with him. And so, he soon found himself standing over a reduced-price sale bin of largely gauche and loud ties, ties that had not sold. In the Prof's lexicon, these were "remaindered" ties, or ties (like books) that would not sell. Certainly he must consider buying one before finding his way to the Electric Shack. He doubted that even he could countenance conducting the annual induction of the new members of the Quinlan University Junior-Senior Honor Society, for which he was faculty moderator, wearing the same tie for the 21st year in a row. Two decades of the beige slim-trim tie, circa 1965, purchased he could not remember when or where, had long ago begun to wear on people. (It may have been that it fell off, or was ripped off, the neck of an anti-Vietnam War protestor. Prof Gary liked to hang on the edges of protest rallies to see if any loose coins came loose. A tie might've been one afternoon's consolation prize. He honestly couldn't recall.) His detractors had begun to maliciously take the measure of his dingy, out-of-date neckwear, attributing to him a non-funky tapioca style and persona. He felt a pang of remorse. He should be more savvy to the sensibilities and gossip of the campus community in the hallowed halls, under clinging ivy, of ol' Quinlan U!

He began to hum the school song: "Hail to the mascot, Hail to the mascot, in our hallowed halls..." The refrain four lines later, he had written in a winning entry in a University-wide contest: "Do not lose heart, dear Saint, even when twilight falls." He felt all school songs should end with "twilight falls." Combining this with what he thought sounded like white hip-hop, he came up with his winner and a $100 gift certificate at the QU bookstore.

Prof Gary picked out an ersatz foulard, paisley pattern, a swirl of robin's egg blue and navy blue. He held it up to his chest and examined it. It seemed sedate enough; nothing to get anybody riled, especially QU President Marvin Dillwood. "Dill" could get pretty ticked off if you ran afoul of his conservative interpretation of the university dress code. Not only did faculty have to wear a tie, the tie had to be in "good taste." Which translated as "Prez Dill's good taste," and that meant attire appropriate for a funeral. This one for a buck-99 seemed to meet the criterion. It might just be a safe tie to buy. But maybe there was something safer. Or maybe he should buy two safe ties and alternate them, to spiff up his beige humdrum image. Or maybe he could buy five ties at a buck-99 each and wear a different one for each weekday. That would really trip the light fantastic, and transform the general image of him. This could really be a good investment, this, the bargain bin at—Prof Gary glanced up at a sign—"Jim's Haute Couture Discount Den."

The professor switched from humming to singing under his breath, the Quinlan University school song. He hit the vocal hammer on "under hallowed halls" from the first line, and "when twilight falls," which ended every stanza. His body was moving rhythmically in white hip-hop fashion over the bargain barrel of once fashionable "nooses," his term for ties. He must really be happy, he thought, to sing the Quinlan U song as he examined self-esteem upgrades from among a barrel of ties. He ought to get out of his office more often like this!

Why not splurge? Hell, he was 64, and needed to enjoy life more. Sprucing himself up could be part of that. He should do more than just take a summer trip to Norway to do genealogy research, largely by taking rubbings of tombstones and researching church records harking back to the Middle Ages. He should do more than that. That suddenly struck him as morbid! After all, there was his life to consider, too, in the now and present. Prof Gary gave an involuntary slap to his forehead. "I should've thought of this before," he thought. "It is truly amazing how something mundane like a barrel of discount ties can jog your values in the correct direction! Why just look at the primary, innate beauty of that leghorn noose!..."

THIRTEEN

On the second tier of the mall, two Quinlan University students, Glen and Marcy, were out on a date. They sat in a cozy plastic cubicle at Chez Quinlan, drinking colas, as they waited for their 7:45 pm movie in the SuperPlex. While they waited, they observed Prof Gary trying on ties from the discount-store bin below, savoring the fact that, from their vantage point, they could see the Professor but he could not see them, even if he happened to look up. Perhaps watching the unpredictable professor would be even better than the x-rated movie, "Burning Buns," that they would soon see, featuring the porn star Tina Bunsure. Better in a different way, for sure, yet possibly better for sheer, local entertainment value.

"D'you see Prof Gary, down there?" asked Marcy.

Long Dark River Casino

"Yeah, I see him," replied Glen. "What a dickhead! How many times have we seen him buy el cheapo stuff here."

"Stuff that no one else wants," chimed in Marcy.

"He's tried on a good dozen of them," observed Glen. "Can't he make up his mind?"

"Probably," said Marcy. "After all, he can't even make up his mind on a grade. Every paper I get back from him has four or five grades on it. He has crossed out all of them, except one. I guess it is painful for him to grade us."

Glen scratched at his tattoo of the Quinlan U mascot, a big Saint* Bernard dog. "Yeah, y'know, it wouldn't be so bad if one grade wasn't 72 and the other 92, with two or three in between." He took a sip of his cola. "That guy is something else on his grading."

*Quinlan U teams were "The Saints," a misnomer, for the devilish men's basketball and baseball teams that traveled with large boxes of condoms. By way of contrast, the soccer team traveled sans condoms. This may have had something to do with the fact that the soccer players were the only Quinlan team to travel without their iPods, and so, instead of listening to music on the bus in splendid isolation, they enjoyed lively conversations among themselves. Sad to say, the basketball and baseball players listened to sexually explicit music, each seated alone. So, when they reached Iowa Wesleyan or Upper Iowa University or whatever other conference opponent they were scheduled for, they arrived definitely not ready to play a competitive sporting event.

The upshot was that the two teams together had not won a road game in three years, as compared to the soccer team, which was well above .500 on the road.

*As for the women's teams, information may be revealed as this book develops, and as information becomes available...

Fourteen

Prof Gary finally selected a single subdued paisley tie that swirled together, noncommittally, hues of semigloss, cyanide blue, and terra cotta. "This is me!" he thought, "a noncommittal mélange of offwhite, blue, and drab. That's me! Who can get twerked off by this if I keep it clean of gravy stains!"

The Prof got the feeling he was being watched. Vaguely. But he shook it off. After all, this was the famous Quinlan Mall, where people-watching was one of the main activities of the large number of retired people in the city. They fended off Alzheimer's by coming to the mall to stimulate their fading brains by staring. The Alzheimer's challenged were parked here for hours at a time, to take in the passing scene. Their caretakers had conveniently wheeled them along as a part of their own shopping expeditions. In fact, the area around the multi-colored water fountain in the center of the mall was often referred to as "the Lourdes of Iowa." The dementia-stricken took the waters there, at least visually, as a symphonic liquid display timed to various famous pieces, especially Beethoven's Fifth Symphony and Ravel's "Bolero," played dramatically. Bolero was a piece that seemed positively therapeutic for wheelchair-bound patients with a dementia. He glanced around. Perhaps he was being observed by one or more of these daily habitués of Quinlan Mall. But he saw no one whose line of sight was upon him.

Prof Gary paid for one tie, his final selection. He wheeled abruptly on his heel, because he felt really good about his wardrobe enhancement, and proceeded down the concourse. The last rays of a late sunset were slanting in from the clerestory above. (Spring commencement was but two weeks away!) The sun, suffusing its rays across the aluminum, glass, and tile angles of the mall, created beauty, true beauty. He was here as much for that beauty as he was for shopping and people watching. Who said that the consumer culture could not create its own cathedrals. Pshaw. This mall, this beauteous mall, was one of those cathedrals to prosperity. The glory of the sun ambered succulently through wide and narrow spaces. The Prof even imagined cherubs looking down in approval from pendentives in the ceiling. He felt himself having a Maslowian "peak experience," aka an epiphany.

Thus buoyed up, he came to an area where a card table had been set up. He could see behind one, Quinlan U student, Megan, handing out environmental literature and talking with a stout woman. He paused nearby, shielded by a big plastic schefflera plant in a huge dun-colored ceramic pot. The pot was like a magnet to him, brandishing his favorite color as it did. And, yes, the "green" student on the other side of the forest-green polymer was a draw, too.

He listened. He was up for this. His ears perked up. Megan was into an environmental thing consistent with Quinlan U's mission statement. That mission included inculcating into youth a respect for the biosphere. And here he was witness to the effectiveness of that part of his university's mission. He whipped out of his back pocket a small spiral notebook, set down the shopping bag containing his tie at the base of the faux schefflera, and began taking notes. After all, he was part of the U's "Assessment Committee," charged with collecting data on mission effectiveness. And the heat was on for good data, anecdotal and quantitative, because "The HLC" (initialism for Higher Learning Commission) would visit campus for Quinlan's accreditation evaluation next fall. They hadn't visited for ten years, and this visit was big-time stuff for everyone, faculty and staff, not to mention the students who had been kept thoroughly abreast of the "HLC process" and its critical importance to them. After all, without accreditation, Quinlan could award no degrees.

He began to scribble as he listened intently.

Fifteen

Megan eyed the stout, frumpy, middle-aged woman, clad in a dowdy Dalmatian house dress—black spots on a field of white. She wore house slippers and something on her head that might be a shower cap. Apparently, this trip to the mall was a spur of the moment thing. "I can't help you there," said Megan to the beslippered woman, a bit of annoyance in her tone.

The frumpy dowdy put her hands on her hips, glaring. "Well, you can't tell me that my husband Ernie's employer is polluting the Mississippi River. Iowa Plastics has a clean record on the environment, doncha know?"

Megan retorted, "No, I don't know." Then seeing the escalated tension in Ernie's wife, she smiled appeasingly and made a tidy pile of one each of the information sheets atop the table, and handed it to the woman. "I think Iowa Plastics is a fine employer," she

Long Dark River Casino

soothed. "I'm only here to try to help. If you read this material, you might be able to see how all the companies in Quinlan can come together to make the environment, especially the Mississippi, even cleaner." The woman relaxed her arms to her sides. Some hostility was leaving her.

Prof Gary wrote: "Environmental information provided woman at info table. Woman accepts several fact sheets…Conflict resolution being achieved by Quinlan U student, Megan, at 7:16 p.m., on first concourse of mall. Reflects partial achievement of course objective for Peacemaking class as well as university-wide goal of producing societal peace via our students… Confrontation with local woman averted in the noble cause of meeting her humanity with humanity. No reprise here of Israeli-Palestinian standoff!" He got so excited with what he was writing that he broke his pencil lead. Quickly, he pulled out a pen from his trousers and resumed writing, hunkered behind the plastic schefflera plant.

He poised his pen to write more. But the woman had left. He could see her Dalmatian backside receding into the mall as she padded toward getting a new shower curtain or whatever she was after. It would preferably be, he was sure, a product of Ernie's employer, Iowa Plastics.

A thought occurred to the professor: Did Iowa Plastics make the condoms that were carried on road trips by the Quinlan basketball and baseball teams? If so, were they reliable? Were they also valid? And what rubrics to apply? All these Assessment Committee terms criss-crossed his agitated mind...

Sixteen

Prof Gary stopped by the mall newsstand to buy the local **Quinlan Quotient.** He always got a kick out of the obituaries and wedding announcements. Every obit and every wedding announcement that wasn't his was a small victory. In both categories of small wins, some of the photos struck him as downright gross. And he always read Dr. Paul Donohue's column that answered reader letters on health issues. He had read Dr. Paul so faithfully for so long that he felt he had become a kind of unaccredited health expert. He took copious notes on what Dr. Paul wrote and ceaselessly went over his notes, out of both academic habit as well as his studious concern for his health. For example, from the newspaper guru, he had learned how to compute his bmi, or body mass index. At 202 pounds, his bmi was 25.85, far below the 30 where real obesity began. He liked those numbers, for he knew that without a body to contain his Ph.D. mind and his 40 years of teaching experience and extended study, he could not remain on the Quinlan faculty. For he would be cremains, spread from a helicopter by his lawyer nephew Jesse over the Sierra foothills around Oroville, California where he had grown up and to which he had returned like a pilgrim, righteously, at least once a year ever since he had graduated from Oroville Union High School. Thus, his health was a prime desideratum, an essential to his continuing to nibble the green, green grass of academe.

He handed the news vendor, "Semper Fi," a dollar for the paper. Semper Fi, whose nickname owed to his service as a U.S. Marine, handed him his change.

"How's business?" asked the Prof.

"Can't complain."

"Any big news?"

Semper Fi directed a lop-sided downturned expression toward the paper, pointing at the banner headline: "Tanker Car Runs Off Tracks, Downtown Quinlan!" The sub-caption read: "Toxic Fumes May Have Escaped."

Prof Gary thought back quickly to Megan and her environmental information table. This bad news was something she could use to recruit more citizens onto her bandwagon. He'd have to stop by on the way out and give her his copy of the paper, once he had read it in the No Me Digas Coffee Shop, a shop that catered to the multicultural diversity of Iowa (which is 2.3 percent Hispanic by official count, and maybe up to 4%

Hispanic when the undocumented are factored in as best as possible through statistical analysis).

He cursorily read the lead to the article. "Looks bad," he intoned. "Anyone hurt?"

"Not directly, least not so far. You never know about chemicals."

"Indeed. Perchlorate can take a long time to get you, if the dose is dilute."

Semper Fi nodded as if the full weight of the tanker car capsizing was pressing down on his shoulders.

"This could really hurt the city," said the Prof. "The publicity over a toxic spill could be a killer for admissions to the university. And that would really hurt the city. Students are like four-year tourists. They come, they spend, they leave." Prof Gary thought: Yeah. After we take their money, they leave.

"Well," Semper Fi droned drolly, "the spill could be good for the funeral business."

Prof Gary looked askance at the vendor and thought: You, sir, are a natural-born sicko, aren't you? You like death. You view it as economic growth. You are one sick dude! But he did not speak his thoughts. What he said was, "I enjoyed talking with you today. Peace." Never be provoked into departing the path of peace. Address the humanity of each person you encounter and you will have a successful mall visit....

SEVENTEEN

The director of the Quinlan U library, Dora Dromgoole, surveyed her domain, the shelves that held thousands of rare and semi-rare books as well as the more numerous books for regular student checkout, to inform term papers and senior and masters' theses. She looked to her assistant, Lib Door, and sighed in satisfaction. "It's a great collection, built basically from scratch."

Lib nodded, a simpatico satisfaction curling the corners of her mouth. "Yes, we did it. What a fine library we built."

Dora looked hard at Lib, who amended, "**You** built."

The director smiled magnanimously, for she knew who she was and what she had accomplished, solo and in spite of all the countervailing forces, who had kept marching at her in serried ranks over the years, trying

Long Dark River Casino

to prevent her from building one of America's premier libraries. They didn't call her Dora the Komodo Dragon for nothing. She had shown the naysayers what could be done. And recently, the Midwest Librarians' Association had given her its highest accolade, a Golden Book, the book world's analogue for the movie world's Golden Globe. Dora had arrived, and she was proud of her high achievement. Who would have thought, growing up in dullsville Virginia, she would have reached this pinnacle of excellence? Certainly not her third-grade teacher, Miss Bird, who had predicted the girls' reformatory outside Fredericksburg for her after she had twisted a mass of bubblegum into her friend Shelley's flowing tresses. Well, long-ago-deceased Laurie Bird, you can't predict anything from a normal kid prank, can you? Dora sniffed a kind of victory sniff, her gaze angled toward the vermiculite ceiling of the first floor of the library upon which her broad office window, above her West Virginia marble-topped desk, opened.

Dora's forehead crinkled in remembrance of a forgotten detail. "By the way, have you accessioned Prof Gary's latest book, **The Social Phenomenology of Escargots**? He needs to have it available for his students in the special topics class, **Socially Straight and Stupid Thinking**."

Lib smiled, "I'm doing that now."

"Now! How about yesterday?" Dora shrilled.

Lib bent over Prof Gary's book, assiduously pasting the barcode label for checking out the thin, "insightful"—according to the Quinlan University Press dust jacket—volume on two-hour reserve. She said nothing, ducking conversation. Body language and work were the best idioms at this early 9 a.m. point in her day. She had to pace herself. For, indeed and forsooth, it would be over eight hours before she could get back to the safe haven of her home, husband, and Blue Heeler hound, the family pet, at least two of three which loved her and gave her a refuge from the rigors of her job....

Eighteen

The next day, in the early afternoon, Prof Gary deposited his new paisley tie on his desk. It was nice to get back to campus. The students were streaming down the hall, to go to the next class, or to their residence halls or apartments, or maybe a sweated job in a factory or store. (One or two might even wander into the library to read the assignment for **Socially Straight and Stupid Thinking**.) He liked the rhythm of the Quinlan campus more than the ebb and flow of the mall. Here the cycles were geared to learning and—alas!—a good deal to sports teams, too. Actually, today, the baseball team was just now getting onto the university bus to travel to Waldorf College for a doubleheader. He looked out his third-floor window in Old Main and could see their young solid muscular bodies boarding. The team manager carried two sizable cardboard boxes: one contained baseballs made in Costa

Rica. The other contained a lot of condoms, made in China, that had become more a fetish commodity than a functional one. Everyone had an iPod playing, and, from the moment they boarded, they would all be utterly individually alone, listening to 50 Cent, Snoop Dogg, Beyonce, Madonna, or whoever else was a chart-topper. They would be encapsulated in two types of fantasies: one sexual, the other pertaining to winning a baseball game. Neither fantasy ever seemed to materialize. About as close as they got to satisfaction was post-game pizza paid for by the University. Prof Gary chuckled aloud, "Cold pizza," drawing the glance of a young woman passing his office door.

Of course, it was Quinlan A-Plus Pizza, another one of the products produced and marketed by the large holding company, Big Quinlan, Inc, the powerful mega-corporation whose bottom line eclipsed the GDPs of Nigeria, Colombia, and Argentina **combined.**

That coed that just glanced in here, she likes my tie! surmised the Prof. I am glad I bought that tie. Then a thought struck him: Maybe I should take it out of its bag!

Nineteen

The Prof had an appointment with a student to do something. Just what was it? Register him. Yes, it was a he. He scratched his head...But it wasn't a registration...Oh, yes, there it is, penciled onto the calendar for April 24: "Senior Thesis, Jim Trix." He glanced at his watch. It's almost 2 p.m. He should be here any moment. He's writing some crap about global warming so he can get out of here. Maybe I can get him going so he can at least get the minimum C- to complete the requirement. He should be able to do B or better work. He's bright enough, just not motivated enough...Besides, I'm getting tired of his hanging around my neck like a deceased red-tailed hawk. This is his third try at the senior thesis, and he is wearing on me!

A tall, gaunt young man wearing a gold-on-blue Quinlan U shirt appeared at the doorway, smiling sheepishly. "I didn't get as much done as I'd hoped," he confessed.

The Prof wanted to say something nasty, but in the interest of retention and conflict resolution, he purred, "That's OK. Your full-time job, wife, three kids, not to mention your full-time academic load, might just have a tad to do with it."

Jim Trix smirked. He'd elicited the response he wanted and expected. Prof Gary was such a wonderful man. The faculty and staff at Quinlan were all such nice people! They knew how to address the humanity of a student…

Twenty

The Academic Dean, Caleb High, was sunk deep into his padded swivel chair, holding a Dean's Council meeting. Arrayed before him were the chairs of the various departments in his academic dominion. *They are such obsequious little ne'er-do-wells,* he thought. *I hope none of them falls off his or her chair today for failure of a backbone!*

The assembled were chatting desultorily among themselves, waiting for the meeting to begin. They were talking about the capsized tanker car and how it could dampen enrollment, and maybe even impair their own health. Enrollment was already so low that skeletal budgets had to be revised downward. Toxic fumes could chase applicants away and, in a worst case scenario, kill young local people who were among Quinlan's prospective students.

G. Louis Heath

For his part, Caleb High, Ph.D., was relishing the soothing influence of staring at the framed photo of his peanut-colored Welsh corgi, Quinlan Rex. Just doing so calmed the waters of his soul, making it possible for him to conduct a meeting with equanimity and good cheer.

Soon he cleared his throat, quite audibly. "Meeting called to order," he began. "Who has the opening reflection for today?"

"I do," replied Dr. Phil Woodside, Professor of Anthropology. "I have been visiting an Amish community, about 90 miles east of here, doing ethnographic research, and I wanted to share with you what they have to say about 'graven images,' about the pitfalls of taking photographs of people, of setting up false icons in order to, in effect, worship--"

Dr. High lost the cool that gazing at the photo of his dog had just given him. He interrupted, "Do you realize, Phil, that we are an online campus that makes the bulk of its living through electronic pictures? How can we have a reflection about graven images? Isn't that hypocritical?"

Dr. Woodside flushed. He did not like his opening reflection interrupted, not at all.

Into the void jumped Mary Schroeder, Chair of the Political Science Department, and quite a diplomat. "Let's just skip the opening reflection. I'm sure it's very good. I move we skip the O. R. and have Phil distribute it by e-mail."

Long Dark River Casino

Dr. High seconded the motion. "Is there any discussion?"

"Before we vote," said Dr. Woodside, "I'd like to know whether we're establishing policy here. Is there now a policy that an Opening Reflection can be interrupted and voted on? If so, this issue should go to the full Faculty Assembly, next meeting, which is tomorrow." He sighed heavily. "I would like to propose the counter-motion that the motion before us be tabled and that we bring up the issue of OR interruptus to the entire faculty." He glowered at everyone. "This indeed is serious stuff, shutting down the meditation and prayer that begins all our meetings."

Bill Ydstie, chair of the History Department, chimed in. "Do we need a simple majority or a two-thirds vote at two consecutive meetings to make this profound structural change in our operations?"

TWENTY ONE

Kathy O'Shea, director of the Quinlan Admissions Team, was conducting a meeting of her recruiters, aka "admissions counselors." They were strategizing the last phase of their year's efforts to recruit a high-quality class for the fall term. The goal was to bring together a diverse group of talents and backgrounds that would spend four years enriching each other's experience, growing together, unfolding their potential toward the best possible results, academic, social, and athletic, not to mention the highest possible ethical and spiritual development. All the counselors wore their brightly bedizened TEAM QUINLAN t-shirts, glittering gold on royal blue.

"Well, whaddya say, gang?" enthused the ebullient Kathy. "How're we doing?" She laughed hysterically her trademark hysterical laugh. Everyone had gotten

Long Dark River Casino

used to it somehow. If you were around a while, you could do that.

Marla Mason, the lead counselor for non-trad admissions, took a slow pull on the straw inserted into her Quinlan A-Plus SuperDrink. She closed her eyes with the sheer pleasure of the liquid bathing her tongue, kissing her throat with passionate Quinlan SuperDrink chemistry, gurgling down her esophagus, making haste to please her stomach. Ah, what a wonderful world, this interconnected world of Quinlan. Big Quinlan met all your needs. There was no need to look elsewhere.

"Are you here?" asked Kathy. "You seem distant somehow, Marla."

"Oh, I'm here alright. Just thinking, about how to get those non-trad numbers up. You know me. Always thinking." She gave a short laugh. "Thinking all the time, just like Elvis' Hound Dog."

None of the other counselors laughed or said anything. All were much younger than middle-aged Mom and M.A. recipient, Marla. It wasn't that they didn't like to laugh. The problem was they did not know what Elvis meant by "Hound Dog." They were part of the iPod generation. The world of the 1950s and 45 rpms eluded them. Sure, they had heard the song. They just had never glommed to what it meant. In fine, they lacked context, visceral context.

Kristin Adams, the Quinlan counselor who trolled Chicagoland for students, put in: "I have been working my area a lot, just like you have yours, Marla. I am doing OK, a little better than last year. But no dramatic increases." She paused significantly, lowering her voice. "The problem is the President's goal is well beyond what we're bringing in."

A nervous murmur arose from the group, anxiety incarnate, prelude to the major depression that would ensue if they did not juice the numbers somehow by fall. Certainly, they collectively thought, their staff could not be sustained with the current productivity. At least for on-ground campus recruitment. On-line, the enrollment was growing rapidly and soon would reach thirty thousand, making Quinlan U the largest private university in Iowa. But that was online. Their charge was real bodies who sat in real chairs in real classes. It was a harder challenge, those warm-body on-campus numbers, because serious logistics were involved—getting the kid and his parents on campus, closing the deal, doing the financial aid package, arranging housing, etc, etc. In short, they had much more to do to achieve success than the e-course admissions reps who worked in teams in 5th floor rooms in Old Main and in a new building constructed just outside Quinlan. They recruited over the globe by phone and computer. Not easy, but, to date, much more cost-efficient than the traditional campus.

So Team Admissions brainstormed, drawing particularly on recent anecdotal evidence from their recruiting trips as well as information provided by prospective students on their applications. Marla vouchsafed her idea first: "I get the impression we need to recruit more in the Criminal Justice area. Many interested students put that down as an area of interest. We need to market that more."

Kathy nodded, smiled, and emitted her trademark hysterical laugh. "Dr. Klemetson will be pleased to hear that," she said. "He has worked hard on keeping that program going through the thin enrollment years. He'll be willing to help us market that. So, will the Academic Dean, Dr. High, who had a big hand in creating the Social and Criminal Justice major." She paused. "It is a unique program, the only one like it in the United States. Focus is on social justice, including victim restitution, rather than just crime and punishment. This kind of program resonates with a lot of prospective students and the law enforcement agencies like to hire the graduates from the program. We are happy about that."

Marla resumed: "Maybe we could advertise the program using our successful graduates. Maybe some sort of brochure, with photos of our grads on the job."

Kristin observed, "I hear they're all over, in all sorts of law enforcement in Illinois and Iowa. One is in forensics at the Illinois crime lab near Joliet. Another is in corrections at the Thomson prison a few miles up the river. A few are with the Iowa DCI, Department of Criminal Investigation." She smiled. "We could develop quite a nice list."

Kathy added, "With Dr. Klemetson's help."

The group all nodded vigorously and began to sing the Quinlan school song, the second stanza: "As somnolence settles upon hallowed halls, The great mascot

patrols Achievement Hall, Sniffing this way and that,
Looking for cold pizza on which twilight falls..."

Twenty Two

Prof Gary wasn't exactly avidly keen about sports at Quinlan. In truth, he wasn't keen at all. But he had come to realize that sports was an important part of the University experience for many. So, he had become a solid supporter of athletics, even going so far as serving as faculty athletic representative to the Midwest Classic Conference and the national organization to which Quinlan subscribed, the National Association for Intercollegiate Athletics. He even attended the occasional sporting event. That evening he would attend the annual student-athlete awards ceremony in the friendly confines of the Muscular Arena in the recently constructed, glass, brick, and steel Happiness Center, the most impressive building on campus, a multiplex of classrooms, offices, a gymnasium, and other athletic facilities. The latter included workout areas furnished with treadmills, rowing machines, elliptical trainers, weights and barbells, as well as state-of-the-art locker rooms. (The Happiness Center stood across the street from the Student Success Center, keeping alive the motif of a purpose-driven life.)

When first constructed, the building had been quite a coup for the university. Made possible by a large initial bequest by a local businessman, the imposing three-story building with indoor oval track on the second floor had made Quinlan a much more competitive institution. Prof Gary looked forward to the awards program there that began in a few minutes.

He left the test he was working on up on his desktop screen, locked his office door, and headed off toward the Happiness Center.

It was a warm April evening, a decided break from the previous week's more wintry weather. It had even snowed a little last week. But this week the climate showed its true vernal side, a changeling behavior that was typically Midwestern, a pattern that revealed itself through all systematically recorded weather history, dating back to the late 1800s. The trees had begun leafing out in earnest, especially the frangipani, locust, birch, and maple. It made Prof Gary feel younger to see the leaves return again. Winter had the opposite effect, provoking always a little SAD, or Seasonal Affective Disorder, in him. Not bad but discernible. Certainly enough that, when his demise came, he preferred shuffling off his mortal coil in the spring, or better yet the summer. Dying in the warm weather struck him as a kind of reaffirmation of life.

Long Dark River Casino

Student-athletes, parents, faculty, and administrators were streaming into the Muscular Arena. Nighthawks swooped through the swaths of sodium-arc luminescence emanating from a row of light standards. Prof Gary got in step with some of the Education profs, with whom he got along well. Perhaps because they were, save one, all women. Women education profs neutralized the small, yet extant alpha-male side to him that male profs with fangs brought out. Dr. Woodside in Anthro was one of those heavier alpha types that seemed to bring out the latent dark male alpha side in him. There were tenterhooks between him and "Woody," and they both were aware they had to be careful around each other, for their own respective goods. Quinlan, an institution dedicated to promoting peace, did not want, nor would it tolerate, its profs engaging in psychological, internecine war against each other. So, peace prevailed, but only in the sense that there was an absence of war. That was the best they could do in creating "peace" because for some reason they had loathed each other from the very first day they had met. The healthy part of the situation was that they recognized they were polar opposites—at least not kindred spirits—and they had worked around that conflict much as a successful ceasefire might work.

As he walked with the gentle Ed profs, Professor Martha Mangione took his forearm and cradled it in the crook of hers as they approached the tall wide doors of the Happiness Center. She smiled brightly at him and his dark thoughts about Woodside subsided.

"Two of my advisees are up for awards tonight," she enthused. "I hope they get them."

Prof Gary returned her enthusiasm. "I know one of mine that is up for a soccer award. Lee Angstrom. I call him the Big Swede. He had a good year as midfielder. I think he deserves something."

"I went to most the soccer matches, and I agree," said Martha. "He certainly deserves something."

"Where's your husband, Martha?" asked Prof Gary. "He usually accompanies you."

"Oh that. We are kind of splitsville."

"Oh," said the Prof, disengaging his arm from hers...

Twenty Three

After the athletic awards ceremony, several cars of student-athletes took off for downtown bars to celebrate their most recent rite of passage. They invited Prof. Gary and he followed them to the street on which the Voodoo Lounge stood, not foursquare, but slightly askew. (Since there was no building code in Quinlan, market forces were relied on to keep buildings standing in some semblance of quality and safety.)

The Prof got out of his 1991 rust bucket, a blue Cavalier, which he called "Quisling," after the Norwegian dictator who betrayed his people by ruling Norway for Hitler from 1941 to 1945. In parallel fashion, this latter-day car Quisling had betrayed him rather often, leaving him in the lurch, without transportation, especially when Alberta Clippers swept down from Canada or when the rain descended in teeming sheets. Just as the death penalty had been imposed on the historical Vidkun Quisling, there would come a day when the blue Cavalier Quisling would have to be put down, executed for all its betrayals. But this evening, it had done its job, fetching him up at the nefarious Voodoo, site of many a drunken brawl and police intervention as chronicled in the **Quinlan Quotient** and the word-of-mouth municipal grapevine.

The Prof managed to get the rusty driver's side door closed and locked on the third try. Feeling good about that, he pivoted with alacrity on the heels of his 13-B black Knapp sensible shoes and strode purposefully toward the Voodoo, devoutly hoping that there would be no drunken fisticuffs tonight. That's all his 64-year-old face needed, was a steroid-and-booze-bolstered punch in the chops from a powerful young exponent of the Quinlan U athletic world. He feared one of them might pull something. Throw a punch, albeit a mock one. But even a mock punch could go drunkenly awry and injure.

Why might one of them do something playful, yet daunting? They all knew he had challenged George Foreman to a fight for the royalties to his famous barbecue grill. But that was years ago, when Quinlan U was desperate for money to build some sort of endowment, as an anchor to windward. He had had glorious visions of another Kinshasa "Rumble In The Jungle" type of historic match. He was, of course delusional,

Long Dark River Casino

even at the then relatively young age of 51—close to Foreman's. When the Foreman camp started advertising the "Quarrel In Quinlan" match, he was thrown back into reality, becoming positively alarmed. Trembling, paralyzed with fear, he picked up the phone and managed to communicate that the Klemetson vs. Foreman "Quake At QU" match (the other traumatic catchphrase the advertising used) had to be cancelled. He could not remember the excuse he gave. He was that frozen with fear. Perhaps he had gone so far as to say he was dying of terminal cancer. He could not recall. Nor did he care. Just so Foreman kept his grill and he kept his life. Yet the figurative aroma and smoke of that grill kept circulating in his life, year after year, threatening in an unguarded moment to unsettle him.

Just before he pulled open the door to the Voodoo, Dr. Gary muttered to himself, "I don't think I am going to have a philosophical discussion about Ludwig Wittgenstein's **Tractatus Logico-Philosophicus** in here. No way!" Thus self-forewarned, he entered the portals of the Voodoo, Quinlan's most iniquitous and loud watering hole. The very walls seemed to undulate to the throbbing music—a kind of techno-booming hip-hop, as best as he could construe. No "hallowed halls…twilight falls" kiddy treacle here. This was hardcore boombox stuff that was threatening to split his tympani, boding ill to snuff out his livelihood that depended on his being able to hear student questions and participate effectively in committee work.

Lee Angstrom, who had won the award as best soccer player, greeted him very friendlily. "Hi Doc. Glad you could make it. Here's a beer for you."

Almost involuntarily, similar to a knee reflex, he said, "Oh thank you. Thank you very much," even though he never drank alcoholic beverages. To him, they should be made illegal, as they were just as bad as heroin and cocaine and over-the-counter prescription disasters such as Actiq, some forty times more potent than heroin. So, he just took the glass of beer as graciously as he could, hoping the poor light in the bar hid his grimace. He sucked occasionally on the lip of the glass, imbibing no beer, so as to fit into the scene for the few minutes he intended to stay. How he got conned into being here he could not fathom now. Certainly, it ranked as one of his weaker moments. He should be back in his office at his computer, completing the final exam for the Sociology of Sport class he taught to these hulking muscleheads.

Tina Lincoln certainly caught him by surprise. She came out of the shadows and clinked glasses with him. Maybe she'd had a couple quick ones that made her go beyond the bounds of decorum. "Wanna piece of me?" she asked Prof Gary.

"Wanna throw darts?" returned the Prof. "I'm good at that. Darts is my kinda thing. I don't know piece from puce."

"OK, let's throw darts," acquiesced Tina. "Dr. Klemetson says darts is his game. Let's give him a whirl on that, gang." She spoke very loudly, and the Quinlan people in the Voodoo began applauding, not because they understood what she had said, but because she had said something loud that must be important enough to applaud. Besides, when you're getting drunk, you tend to applaud just to applaud. It's what you do when your mood is enhanced by alcohol and you are boisterous in the aftermath of a major athletic awards event.

Tina and Prof Gary squared off in dramatic fashion at the regulation distance from the cork board, divided into colored slices, representing a range of point values, all slices culminating in the bull's eye, which was worth the most, 50 points. There was a scuffed white line—it looked like athletic trainer's tape that had been laid down—to mark where you had to toe as you launched a dart. Almost all eyes were upon them, and the athletes gathered like warthogs around a waterhole, ugly and thirsty, a kind of mob for whom chug-a-lugged beer served as an added stimulus to testosterone arising.

Tina went first. She was a leftie with a sidearm delivery, forcing Prof Gary to move to her right side, where he, a rightie with a steep overhand delivery, could be most effective. This was a duel that featured quite a disparity in the ages of the participants; over forty years. Just how did he get himself into this? This could be embarrassing. He had not thrown a dart in over twenty years. He did, however, keep in shape, and maybe his devotion to good health would help him here. That, plus his glasses, highly corrective in the right eye, might enable him to achieve a face-saving score.

G. Louis Heath

Tina flung her first dart. It missed the cork board, though not by much. It stuck in the Marlite wall just below a clock advertising Leinenkugel Beer, one of the favorite libations in eastern Iowa. "Darn!" screeched Tina. "Darn, darn, darn. I should take more time."

She took a prolonged time to study her next toss, focusing her mind, letting her beer perspire on a nearby table. It seemed like Zen darts the way she comported herself on her second toss—a big contrast to the run-up to her initial dart. She even closed her eyes a few seconds, visualizing a successful toss. Then she opened her eyes, and threw the dart. This one stuck in the cork, in a red portion of the 16-point sector, close to the bull's eye, a "trip 16," worth 48 points.

It was a very nice shot, and Tina garnered a smattering of applause.

Now it was tension time, cut-to-the-chase, cut-to-the-quick, nail-biting time for Prof Gary. Sweat glimmered on his forehead. He took his time, surveying the board, to see where a dart could score the most points. A "trip 20"—triple the 20-point sector—was worth 60 points, even more than an outright bull's-eye.

Lee Angstrom shouted encouragement. "Do it, Prof Gary. Do it!"

Gary glanced at Lee, smiling weakly. "That is exactly what I intend to do," he said under his breath. "Do it." He mopped his brow with a paper napkin in slow deliberative motions.

Then, with a dramatic windup, which was mostly flourish for the Quinlan students' entertainment, he hurled the dart at the board. But he missed, and missed badly, hitting the big Leinenkugel clock and cracking it. "I missed," he said meekly. "And I broke the clock."

The Quinlan students thought that this was so funny that they joined in a loud round of applause. Prof Gary saw the ludicrousness of the applause, and broke into a wide sheepish grin. "The next one will be a bull's eye," he advised. "Just watch me!"

With a Major League Baseball windup that would do any starting rotation proud, he let loose with his best fast dart. This one, mercifully, found cork, in the 18-point sector. It was a "trip 18" for 54 points, beating Tina's 48. Relieved, Prof Gary threw up his hands and did a victory jig. He was relieved. He had scored. That first shot was a true embarrassment for which he needed to offer to pay. He didn't want to get arrested for vandalizing a clock, even if the damage was wrought inadvertently. "I'll pay for the damage!" Doc Gary shouted to Warren, the barkeep.

"OK," Warren replied. "Jus' leave your address and phone number on the way out and we'll send you the bill."

Prof Gary grimaced inwardly. He was hoping that Warren—who, after all, had once taken a night course from him—would be magnanimous and forgiving, that he would say it was just one of those things, and the insurance would cover it. But no such luck. On his salary at Quinlan, he could not afford to break more than one of anything.

He was deep into the process of getting himself psyched for a second round of tosses, theatrically unlimbering his throwing hand, getting the kinks ironed out prior to The Big Toss. "This is the round that counts," he said in a gravelly voice. "The winner gets a free pitcher of Leinenkugel."

Lee Angstrom stepped forward eagerly. "I'll try," he said matter-of-factly. "I like this sort of thing. Great fun."

Indeed, Lee was no slouch. He defeated Prof Gary handily, winning the pitcher of Leinenkugel. He busied himself chug-a-lugging the beer down as the Prof wrote out his home address on a napkin and gave it to Warren prior to leaving for home. He figured he might be out a good hundred dollars because of a stupid dart game.

Outside, the nighthawks had given up working the sky. Prof Gary missed their intermittent beeping on the wing as well as the display of their dramatic insect-catching skills.

On the way home, Prof Gary picked up a few groceries. It was almost 1:30 a.m. He glanced at his watch. It was exactly 1:30 a.m...

Twenty Four

The next afternoon, Prof Gary arrived at his office about an hour prior to his 11 a.m. class. He wanted to take care of a few course details and check his e-mail before lecturing to his Crime and Society class. Lately crime had been on his mind more than usual. That harrowing experience last night at the Voodo! Though the Quinlan U student-athletes were a wholesome enough crowd, as bar crowds go, something of the reputation and dark ambience of the Voodoo had settled onto his mind, prickling it the past few hours. It was an ominous sensation, though, in point of hard fact, Prof Gary knew of nothing to be particularly worried about—except life and all its vulnerabilities. What was it that Hegel said: We are all actors and objects. We can manipulate our world, but we are also integrally part of the real world, with a body and mind that can be acted upon as well as playing the role of actor, causing change in the world.

G. Louis Heath

The general unease that we can be an object, that is, a victim, and ultimately are destined to die, is pervasive. So, said Wilhelm Friedrich Hegel, the greatest German philosopher of his era. Thus, thought Prof Gary, my sense of discomfort this morning, my malaise, is just part of the human condition. It does not relate to the Voodoo Lounge last night or anything specific.

With those thoughts, Prof Gary tidied his desk and booted up his computer. He felt better. It wasn't till later that he would find that he should have heeded the vibes that were sending him bad omens, rather than gloss them over with self-therapizing pop Hegelianism. He was getting signals from the darker side of reality that he found convenient to discount and shunt aside as best he could. Not smart.

The Prof scrolled down his e-mail. There were a good 20 e-mails this morning. Some was intramural stuff about meetings, on-campus speakers, the usual dither and dross. But was there anything compelling that required his immediate attention? The usual humanitarian stuff about who was going to be executed and where and when in the USA beamed from his screen, urging him to pray. Six were going to be "murdered by the state" this week. Actually, he had long since gotten tired of these death penalty alerts. Not so much that he didn't care. He did. The death penalty is bad. But the procession over the years of announcements of each and every execution had made him so numb that seldom did he now read an alert. Rather, he most often routinely deleted them, so as to avert the pain of them.

He disliked the helpless pinwheeling rage reading all of them engendered. Climbing onto the cross of social consciousness had long ago ceased being his number one priority. He had become pragmatic, and he hoped more effective, going mainstream, contributing his yeoman bit to established foundations, charities, and political causes. That kept him out of harm's way and was arguably more effective.

Ever since he protested a troop train during the Vietnam War when he was a student at Berkeley, he had increasingly recoiled from direct action. Yes, he had escaped injury, rolling off the tracks just in time. But the guy sitting-in next to him, had not been so nimble and had lost a leg (as well as some spare change). Prof Gary shook his head. Was it worth it? He exhaled forcefully, crimping his forehead in furious, angry thought. He seriously doubted it, and he wondered what had happened to that guy, Sonny Watson, the amputee of that fateful cerulean Oakland, California day. If he knew where he lived, he'd return his pocket change.

He had more e-mail and e-junk than usual for mid-week. What was going on? Why the change? E-mail begets e-mail, and he had been procreating his share lately. Maybe he should cut back.

He stopped scrolling at the e-mail tagged "Lee Angstrom Thanks you." What could that soccer icon be thanking me for? He opened it and read:

Dear Prof G,

I really appreciate that you thought enough of the soccer team to attend the annual sports awards ceremony. I know you don't go to a lot of events like this, so I was real proud you came to this one. My award means a lot to me.

Who knows what the future holds? -- Some good. Some bad. I hope the bad doesn't win out completely soon. If you know what I mean?

Best,

Lee

Prof Gary scratched his head. That is quite a message, he thought. Is it just amorphous or is it cryptic, full of hidden meaning? It imparts a fateful bad feeling. Demons and omens seem to lurk within. Or is my imagination overactive this morning? Perhaps I should've gotten a better night's sleep. He stifled a yawn. Five hours are probably too little, putting my mind on edge.

Next e-mail please. The secretary, Sadie, is now a grandmother. Her daughter, Sheila just had an eight-pound boy. And the Prof added aloud under his breath: "They are trying to locate the father to tell him his new status in life and to get some child support out of the bozo." Ha, ha. That is so unfunny. Get a life, G!

But don't get a death (which is soon coming your way).

Off to class. Knock 'em dead.

Twenty Five

The next Monday morning, death was there: recumbent, splayed across his desk, naked, the **rigor livor** genitals lollygagging grotesquely over a yellow notepad onto which he had been doodling, beginning to write one of his "philosophical poems." Best to finish my poem before I deal with the last remains of Lee Angstrom, third-generation Swede, he thought.

The muse in the Prof waxed ink onto the pad:
Here lies Lee
Star midfielder
Should I call the cops?
Or think on this:
How a naked young man of Swedish descent
Came to fetch up for good on my office desk
Bringing me a murder to solve.
Should the Norsk sleuth go into action
For a Svensk cadaver?

Long Dark River Casino

The Prof read his words, then quickly slid the paper into his desk, and called his friend, Captain Alex O'Gara of the Quinlan P.D. What was he thinking, writing a poem as a body cooled on his desk? He needed to get his priorities right ASAP.

Captain Alex answered the phone. "Alex, this is Dr. Gary up at Quinlan. I got a little something on my desk you need to know about…."

Twenty Six

Captain Alex stood over the body, scratching his head, clipboard grasped in his other hand. "Y'say his name was Lee, doya?"

The Prof nodded, tears welling in his eyes. He had lost all sangfroid and aplomb. Initially, Lee Angstrom was a body, a category he could better wrap his mind around. Now, as **rigor livor** advanced toward **rigor mortis**, his mind had rebelled and he had begun to take in the body as a young man cut down in the prime of life. The gods had struck him into carrion just like that! But not just any carrion, but young human carrion with a soul that had many miles to go on the anatomical odometer. A man. A young man. A Quinlan University student-athlete. And not just any student-athlete, but the true rarity, an intellectually brilliant athlete, in the mold of the 1939 Heisman Trophy winner, the University of Iowa's Nile Kinnick. The words of the appropriate mantra for such premature, tragic deaths blazoned across his mind: Such a waste! Such a waste!...Like a ticker at the bottom of a TV screen.

Finally, Prof Gary pitched his arms wide apart and cried, "Who could've done this?"

Captain Alex eyed the Prof stonily. "Another question is: How did the body end up on your office desk?" He poised a pen over the notepad on his clipboard, prepared to write. "And another question is why?" He wrote down something.

The Prof could not see the writing, nor did he care to. His brain was just beginning to process both the awfulness and the possibilities sprawled before him. Of course, he was acute enough to realize that he himself would have to be on the list of suspects, to be crossed off, once the investigation concluded. He shuddered inwardly. And, indeed, **he** was the only suspect that came immediately to mind! After all, the cooling body between the captain and himself lay recumbent, at ill-sorted, grotesque angles, totally nude on **his** desk, atop a good six inches of **his** paper and book clutter that represented the academic year that was soon to end. (His custom, was to use the summer to file or toss the clutter, to achieve a clean desktop for the fall semester. Usually he succeeded at that task; occasionally he failed.)

Prof G stammered, "I don't have a clue how poor Lee ended up dead on my desk. It seems the height of the ma—ma—macabre to me." He shrugged heavily, the weight of all the brick tonnage of Old Main pushing down on his shoulders. "It looks like a cult murder, or something weird to me." Prof G pointed at the pallid chest of the corpse. "What does that mean?"

"What am I s'posed to see?" asked the captain.

"That tattoo or whatever it is, just below the left pec muscle. It's kind of hidden in the chest hair."

The captain bent over and scrutinized the chest. "Mmmm," he murmured. "Just what is this?" He narrowed his eyes to slits, peering intently. "It's a bird, I think."

The Prof stooped over and looked closely, too. "A red hawk!" he exclaimed. He paused, rubbing his chin in his professorial way, the way he always did in class when he was changing directions in his lectures or simply mulling over what he had just said, waiting for the class to respond. "Yeah, indeed, a red hawk. Could it be a fertility symbol of some sort?"

"On a man?"

"Or maybe a gang logo, if you will," continued the Prof.

The Captain squinted, a brown study. "I'll have Forensics photograph this and run a digital through our data bank. I recall something about hawk symbols being in there. Maybe we can find a match."

The Quinlan P.D. had strung yellow curtilage tape across the hallway to prevent onlookers from getting near the Prof's office. But several of the campus community huddled down the hall, pressed against the tape, straining to hear what was going on. They were there because they had heard what had happened, and like the entire Quinlan U family, had been stunned to the core by the news. Among the gossips at the tape was the secretary, Sadie, the chief grapevine on campus. She knew how to grow juicy grapes with her own very special grafts...

Twenty Seven

Prof G had to get away from campus. Lee's corpse had been removed by the med techs from his office, but he still felt its palpable presence on his desk. His overloaded synapses were driving him crazy! His nerves were jerking him around, causing his emotions to whirl. He was trying to exert a modicum of control over his riled and belabored nerves. He exhaled forcefully. He would not be able to get himself under control in his office. Would he ever? He would forever see the naked corpse of Lee Angstrom piled very dead on his desk each time he entered from now on. Could he change offices? But how to do that? No one in his right mind would want OM (Old Main Hall) #321 now! The only hope would be to clean it thoroughly, sodium hydroxide and bleach at a minimum, and maybe proceed to fumigate it and fob it off on a hapless adjunct in the Liberal Arts, desperate for an office. That might be the ticket. For now, he needed to visit the mall in order to relieve the stresses that were racking him up royally.

The Prof pulled on his Quinlan U cap, donned his Quinlan U windbreaker, and descended the stairs toward the parking lot. On the stairway, he ran into Peggy Lantos, a graduate student, whom he had advised years earlier as the chair of her senior thesis paper on "The Social Stigmas of Sundry, Salient Autoimmune Diseases," an interesting paper, or at least as interesting as a B paper could be.

Peggy flashed her trademark broad smile. "How are you, Professor G?" Her eyes showed concern. "I heard about..." Her voice trailed off, uncertainty slicing off her words.

Professor G nodded solemnly, his eyes brimful of pain. "It's terrible." He shifted his weight from one leg to the other. "A body in my office. It's all so overwhelming. I just have to get out of here."

"Whereya going?"

"The Mall."

"Can I come?"

"I guess so."

Peggy nodded. She knew Prof G was no womanizer, and she felt a sense of obligation to use her Social Science degree with a concentration in Psychology to try to help him out of his mental funk, or whatever he was in. Her literature professor, Gino Belchoni, always referred to funks as "sloughs of despond," borrowing from **Pilgrim's Progress**. Maybe that was what it was, more a metaphor to be borrowed from a lit classic than a category of the DSM IV-TR, the **Diagnostic and Statistical Manual**, 4th edition, Text Revised, published by the APA, the American Psychological Association. With her interdisciplinary quality Quinlan U degree, she might be able to somehow therapize—at least put in appropriate historical literary context—the uniquely interdisciplinarily-concocted Dr. G.

She savored the challenge in her mind's eye. Prof G was about as sexually beguiling as a pinch of Swedish snus. Her pulse-quickening owed to the pursuit of applying her intellectual skills in a real-life scenario, a phrase that was pretty close to a quote from the Quinlan mission statement for the Social Science B.A. She felt a flush of pride, of triumph. Once homeless on the streets of Quinlan, she had climbed out of the gutter of a bad life to become a productive member of society, a well-educated woman who could not only support herself, but whose promise extended to giving back to society in order to help others help themselves. Prof G seemed a good place to do good work at this moment in time. He was her opportunity to serve in the realized present...

Twenty Eight

Prof G drove along Bluff Boulevard toward the Quinlan Mall. The spring day offered dappled sunshine under the spreading shagbark hickories and wide elm, ash, and sassafras trees. A bright yellow goldfinch, Iowa's state bird, liltingly glided onto a honeysuckle bush flanking the road, to post himself for insect-catching duties. Peggy did not see the goldfinch, but she noticed another feature of spring on the windshield: bugs, aka insects.

"You might stop at Quinlan Filler-Up to squeegee your windshield, and top off your tank. This glass is really ugly," she grimaced.

For months, Quinlan had experienced no hint of the life of Arthropoda. Yet, now they had returned with a vengeance, resuming where they had left off when they had been interrupted by the first freezes of autumn. Where there had been a palette of color in the initial freezing time of year, there was now a greening of the landscape that was very uplifting, as if the white and gray and brown prisms through which one had been viewing had been suddenly removed from the eyes.

"I hadn't noticed that," observed the Prof. His face flushed slightly. Though he was often oblivious to such details of life, once they were brought to his attention, he inevitably found them at least disconcerting, if not outright embarrassing.

They stopped at Quinlan Filler-Up (owned, of course, by the global corporate octopus, Quinlan, Inc.) to clean the windshield and self-serve-pump three gallons into "Tormod," Prof G's second nickname for his car, in honor of a second-cousin he'd looked up in Oslo, Norway once. Tormod seemed very musically inclined at that time, in 1965, a young man, like himself. He had done well in his music studies at the conservatory. Unfortunately, he had died in his thirties, victim of a teenager speeding on graduation evening for gymnasia students. In remembrance, Prof G had dubbed his car, 100K plus miles registering on the odometer, "Tormod." On some days, when the Prof was feeling expansive and full of cheer and good will, the car was "Sir Tormod." On bad days, he cursed his creaky conveyance with the hot first epithet, "Quisling!"

Long Dark River Casino

Peggy felt a little inhibited about broaching the topic of the corpse in Prof G's office. Yet, she did not want to participate in an extended denial by gabbing further about the Arthropoda that accumulated on the windshield. She knew that images of Lee Angstrom's body must be darting over the Prof's interior silver screen in a most besetting manner. She wondered: Just how do you psychologically handle a stiffening body, of a student who has taken several classes from you and whom you have gotten to know well, as a person, not just an identifiable presence? That must be very stressful, especially for a self-confessed "true humanist who believes devoutly in God," the Prof's own words, often enunciated at various venues around campus, especially at faculty meetings and in hallway chit-chat.

"I heard the body had a tattoo on it," said Peggy. "Is that true?"

The Prof eyed her, thankful for her candor. That was all his internal monologue was about, that accursed body. Now maybe he could relieve himself of some of the angst and pain of those dreadful images that had seized his brain. Peggy might be a good one to unburden himself to. She had a reputation for not blabbing every wisp of info and gossip that drifted her way. He nodded at Peggy. "Yes, that is true. Deep in the excelsior of his rather substantial chest hair, Captain Alex and I found a tattoo." The Prof paused lengthily, measuring his thoughts, trying to find the right words.

"And?..."

"And what?"

"And what was it like?"

"It was a hawk. A red hawk. Not at all realistic or natural. It was a stylized hawk, something like a logo you might find on a product with a hawk brand name."

Peggy imagined the hawk as best she could, pondering her own response. "It looked like a red-tailed hawk then?"

"It was red, but I don't think any particular species of hawk. It was very stylized. Could have been almost any kind. Even a kestrel or sharp-shinned." He shrugged. "Who knows? Maybe the species is beside the point." He paused as they passed the brick façade of Bluff Elementary School. "Maybe the tattoo, if that's what it is, is not important at all."

"Then it could really be a red herring," quipped Peggy. "Not a red hawk at all."

The Prof slowly presented a lopsided, somber grin, as he drove from the gas station, taking the road that led to the fabled Quinlan Mall three miles away...

Twenty Nine

The soccer team had called an emergency meeting. One of their own had died under mysterious circumstances! Had he been murdered? It surely looked like it, though hearsay had it that no marks of violence marred the corpse. Was Prof G the murderer? If so, how could a bright Ph.D., though aged, be so stupid as to deposit the body on his desk and call the police? "These are some of the things we need to discuss," thought team captain Mahmet Zamodu, an American of Ethiopian-Turkish descent, and leading scorer on the Quinlan Saints soccer team. He had scheduled the meeting for the Energy Room, in Achievement Hall, a residence housing 80 students.

Wisps of cirrus cloud lazed high above against a blue canopy as QU's best sports team, its soccer squad, filed into Achievement, singly and in pairs. They had heard about the tragedy that had befallen their midfielder and good friend, Lee. He had been popular for his laidback easygoing manner and top soccer skills. He was friendly to everyone and provided a lot of glue for a team whose diversity produced a lot of centrifugal force, threatening to drive them apart. Lee provided the centripetal countervailing energy against any serious friction and fracturing.

The team of nine different nationalities, including the Americans, had had to become a successful miniature United Nations in order to be effective. Lee had done his yeoman's share toward that end. And now, tragically, he was dead. The mourning would be intense, exacerbated by the need to fill the void his death created. There did not seem to be anyone on the bench who could serve as such a natural leader. Certainly, no one on the roster rivaled his midfielding talent.

"I called this meeting," announced Mahmet, "to talk." He panned the assembled team with his olive eyes. "You know why we are here. To talk about Lee, to talk about what we need to do."

"And remember him!" chimed in Jorge brightly. Jorge was a forward who had been recruited from Argentina.

A guttural murmur rose from the team, a bass counterpoint to Jorge's brassy chime. The overall mood was subdued, almost reverent, very atypical for the usually irreverent, skylarking team. Most felt Jorge too upbeat in the immediate aftermath of a murder on campus, even though he was only asking for memory.

Long Dark River Casino

"This is the worst day of my life since my sister died in a car crash on Highway 30, traveling to visit me here," said Mahmet. "You guys helped me out a lot then to get me through that." Mahmet saw nods among the team. He held out his open hands as a supplicant. "And now we can help each other again. We must draw together, hang tough together, to get through this." He paused, his dark Turkic eyes panning the team, all of them, in 100 percent attendance and support. Even those who rarely saw action had shown up, answering the tocsin of emergency. He deeply appreciated this solidarity. It made him even prouder to be the Captain of the Quinlan U soccer team. "We must now talk, pool what we know, to see if we can help Captain Alex of the police department. Anything you can think of, even if you think it is not important, bring it up now. It could be very important to the police though you think you saw nothing significant."

Jorge rose. He wore his soccer uniform and his prized New Balance cross-trainers. "I saw Lee at the Voodoo Lounge. That was the last time I saw him." He surveyed his teammates. "Did anyone see him after that?" He sat down onto a drab gray folding chair.

Kevin, he of the red-haired mop, stood, and brushed aside a strand of air that had ranged over his face to cover a hazel eye. "I saw him once this week at the Ashram Tattoo Parlor in the Quinlan Mall. He was sitting in their waiting room. That's all I saw."

Randy put in, "I heard there was a tattoo on Lee's body. Maybe there is a tie-in of that to his death."

Mahmet opined, "Bears looking into. That's one thing we can tell Captain Alex. Are there others?"

"The tattoo could be the key to the murder," observed Kevin. "Does anyone know anything?"

Henri, a player from Trois Rivieres, Quebec, said rather fiercely, "I never saw any tattoo on him when we practiced, shirts off, in the heat. Must be a recent tattoo, no?"

"Must be," concurred Mahmet. "Captain Alex knows there is a tattoo on Lee's body. What we don't know is: why did he get a tattoo? Was it more than just a lark for a free spirit?"

Pedro, the most muscular man on the squad, noted darkly, "Maybe there was poison in the tattoo? I hear people get sick from some of the tattoos they get at the Ashram Tattoo Parlor." He rolled up his sleeve. "I got this beauty there. It made me very sick for a few days." The tattoo glistened redly in the late afternoon, slanting light. It was a stylized red hawk, very similar to, if not identical, to Lee's. But at this point, no one knew that.

The prevailing sentiment of the team was implicit in the tautness of their bodies and guarded looks. **Lee's blood is still warm, and the murderer might even be among us at this very moment!** It was a trepidating thought, to say the least…

Thirty

Prof G and Peggy found a free vinyl-upholstered booth at the Quinlan, Inc Coffee Bar. Prof G liked it here as he got a faculty discount by showing his Quinlan U ID card. And, besides, the coffee was top-notch, organically grown in Honduras and El Salvador, with "fair market" purchases made directly from small farmers to ensure them a viable profit. This made the coffee a little more expensive than cutthroat competitors', but it produced a good deal of economic justice to go with a fine cup of java. That made him feel slightly better, lifting a little of the murk of depression that had settled on him. He still felt so very stunned. He knew that going through the motions of everyday activities, like this coffee shop visit, were the only things that outwardly held him together. Certainly, he had fallen apart inside. The generalized stress of the tragedy that had befallen Lee Angstrom had made him feel uneasy, out of sorts.

It had caused a flush to appear on his neck and cheeks. Probably his blood pressure was way up. He hoped this did not make him look guilty. That would be the cat's meow. Getting accused of something not only he didn't do, but of which he was incapable!

Peggy glanced into the Astral Bookstore that connected to the coffee shop. The Prof followed her glance, saying "We'll go in there after we caffeinate ourselves. There may be a book in there that will help with the investigation." He unloaded from a tray the cups of coffee he had purchased at the coffee bar counter, slightly spilling some of his. "Ooops," he said reflexively, as Peggy leaned forward with a paper napkin to absorb the spillage. "Thanks," he acknowledged, as he joined her in sitting down. He looked deeply into Peggy's brown eyes, looking for a sign that he could fully unburden himself to her. She might be his best hope in this regard, other than his cockatoo, Rigoletto, who never failed to keep his beak shut, but, who, beyond that, was not very useful as a confidant. Peggy had that soothing, feminine touch that he desperately needed, a transference figure onto whose shoulders he could load his cares, much as he used to deposit his worries on his mother's broad shoulders.

Prof Gary peered intently into her eyes and saw the Red Hawk.

About the Author

G. Louis Heath, Ph.D., has served as Professor of Sociology and Criminal Justice at Ashford University in Clinton, Iowa since 1988. He holds B.A., M.A., and Ph.D. degrees from the University of California at Berkeley. He was born in Portola, California in the Western Pacific Railroad Hospital and grew up in Oroville, California, located in the foothills of the Sierra Nevada, at the base of the Feather River Canyon. He worked his way through university as a firefighter for the California Division of Forestry.

Dr. Heath is the author of Harper and Row's bestselling textbook, **The New Teacher.** His volume of short stories, **Meskwaki Burial Mounds and Other Stories from Quinlan, Iowa,** is available in most Iowa libraries. His latest book prior to this one was the 2007 **Harold Sinclair of Illinois: Letters, Biography,** about the famous historical novelist whose works include **Music Out Of Dixie, The Cavalryman,** and **The Horse Soldiers**, the latter made into a 1958 John Wayne movie by the same title.

Long Dark River Casino

NORMANDALE COMMUNITY COLLEGE
LIBRARY
9700 FRANCE AVENUE SOUTH
BLOOMINGTON, MN 55431-4399